What We Save for Last

What
We Save
for Last

Stories by

Corinne Demas Bliss

MILKWEED EDITIONS

WHAT WE SAVE FOR LAST

Milkweed Editions
528 Hennepin Avenue, Suite 505
Minneapolis, Minnesota 55403
Books may be ordered from the above address.

ISBN 0–915943–69–7

95 94 93 92   4 3 2 1

Publication of this book is made possible by grant support from the Literature
Program of the National Endowment for the Arts, the Cowles Media / Star
Tribune Foundation, the Dayton Hudson Foundation for Dayton's and Target
Stores, Ecolab Foundation, the First Bank System Foundation, the General
Mills Foundation, the I. A. O'Shaughnessy Foundation, the Jerome Founda-
tion, The McKnight Foundation, the Andrew W. Mellon Foundation, the
Minnesota State Arts Board through an appropriation by the Minnesota
Legislature, the Northwest Area Foundation, and by the support of generous
individuals.

Library of Congress Cataloging-in-Publication Data

Bliss, Corinne Demas.
    What we save for last : stories / by Corinne Demas Bliss.
      p. cm.
    ISBN 0–915943–69–7 (pbk.)
    I. Title.
  PS3552.L54W43 1992
    813'.54–dc20   91–45688
                                                           CIP

For Matt

Some of the stories in this collection have appeared
in the following publications:

"Babylove," *The Agni Review*

"Birthday Card," *Special Report: Fiction*

"The Dream Broker," *Redbook*

"Ears," *The Boston Review*

"Forbidden Waters," *The Virginia Quarterly Review*

"Headlines," *Michigan Quarterly Review*
(winner of the Lawrence Foundation Prize)

"Luba By Night," *Fiction*

"Margaret, Are You Grieving?" *Mademoiselle*

"Memorial Day," *San Francisco Chronicle, St. Petersburg Times,*
and *Kansas City Star*
(NPR Playhouse: "The Sound of Writing II")
(PEN Syndicated Fiction Competition winner)

"Reparations," *McCall's*

"Small Sins," *Columbia*

"What We Save for Last," *The Providence Journal* Sunday Magazine
and *New England Living*

The author is grateful for support from
The National Endowment for the Arts.

What We Save for Last

Birthday Card   11
Headlines   15
What We Save for Last   27
Babylove   33
Downstream   37
Small Sins   49
Margaret, Are You Grieving?   57
Ears   69
Forbidden Waters   79
Memorial Day   87
Luba by Night   91
Reparations   101
The Dream Broker   107

What We Save for Last

Birthday Card

I heard from a mutual friend that he lives in a walled-off compound with an armed guard at the gate. He's in the Philippines now, and the American company he works for, I'm told, has also assigned him a guard with a gun that shoots real bullets. The guard follows him around as closely as his half-beagle, half-collie did when he was a boy.

This may or may not be true. I have not seen him nor heard his voice for eight years. It has been more than a decade since we have lain together, skin against skin. I cannot even remember the last time. In the final months we were together we quarreled so often, each time we made love threatened to be the last, and now they all blur. Now, the only contact between us is the birthday card he sends me every year. I have a husband he has never met and two children who do not know his name. He has had two wives. I got a glimpse of his first wife, long ago, after a concert in the city. He and I had been only a few rows apart from each other for two symphonies and a concerto, and had not known until we were leaving. My husband had already gone for our car, and I was waiting under the awning. We spoke for only a minute. His wife was wearing a blue-gray dress, a color which I have not been able to look at objectively since. But he was not married to her for long. He met and married his second wife while he was working in Brussels. I don't know if they were together when he was in Africa. I don't know if she went with him to the Far East, if they're still together now.

Today is my birthday, my thirty-fourth. I am alone in the house, waiting for the mailman. When my husband comes home from work, he and my children will make me a cake from the cake mix my daughter has been hiding under her bed, and they will sing "Happy Birthday" to me after dinner. My son has already given me his present, an ashtray he made in ceramics at school. It came out of the kiln three days ago and he couldn't wait. I don't smoke, but I'll use it on my desk to hold paperclips and rubber bands. This morning when I woke up, my daughter had strung the crepe paper across the living room. It has bright yellow letters that spell out an endless string of Happy Birthdays. We bought it years ago for a child's birthday party and it is dutifully unfurled for each of our birthdays every year. My daughter hung it by herself—she is just old enough to do such things. As I sit here with my second cup of coffee, listening for the sound of the mailman's jeep, the masking tape relinquishes its hold on the wall, and the crepe paper flutters down across the sofa, white side up.

I can usually hear the mailman coming half a mile away. I can hear him shift into low gear. I know that if I put on my boots as he starts up the hill, I'll have enough time to get to the end of our driveway when he comes by. Sometimes he's the only person I talk to till the school bus brings the kids home in the afternoon. I'm a free-lance writer—I write articles on nature and rural life. Sometimes I make little forays into the city, but most of the time I am home, unguarded, in a house so quiet that most of the sounds I hear are my own.

The mailman and I have known each other for years, but still we never address each other by name. Our subject matter is limited to town gossip and the weather. I'm sure he knows a lot about me from my mail, but he is scrupulous about never commenting on it. I am sure he knows a manuscript that is coming back, a check from a magazine, a letter from my agent—maybe even a birthday card in an envelope with foreign stamps and postmark that comes, addressed to me, once a year. He hands me my mail—if I'm there when he drives by—with the same detachment as when he leaves it in the box.

The mail is late this morning. I pass the time reading articles I missed in the day-old newspaper and watching a pileated woodpecker in the woods outside my window work away at a dead tree. Perhaps I will write an article about him, this crow-sized bird with a comical red crest. This is the sort of thing I write about: birds, wildflowers, gardens, ponds. The things that give us pleasure but rarely tug at the heart.

When I hear the mailman's jeep finally start up Perkin's hill, I put on my jacket and my boots. Although it's the beginning of April, there's still snow on the ground. Some years, on my birthday, spring has already taken hold. Other years it's winter still. I reach the end of the driveway just as the jeep pulls up. The mailman leans across his seat with my pack of mail and tells me that if I'm planning to drive to town I should take the back road. The electric company is out doing tree work, he says, and they've got part of the main road closed off. He's behind on his route and says a quick good-bye.

I cradle the mail in my arms and walk back up to the house, but I don't let myself look until I've taken off my boots and jacket and am back in the livingroom, in my chair. On top of the pile is my monthly checking account statement. Underneath is an invitation to join the National Geographic Society addressed to my daughter, then a sales announcement from a shoe store, then a request for annual giving from my Alma Mater, and then, on top of a supermarket circular, there is an envelope from him. There are four stamps in the upper right corner, the same profile on each one, three orange, one green. There is no return address. In the center of the envelope is my name and address in his handwriting, a handwriting I recognize as quickly as I recognize my own. He's used a pen with a thick point and black ink. I picture his left hand gripping it as he writes. His fingers are as clear to me as the writing on the envelope. I hold the image right there; I don't give myself any more of him than his hand. I open the envelope carefully, along the flap, and slip my fingers inside. The surface of the card is a glossy paper, stiffer than the envelope. It is, I know, an ordinary birthday card, an American style, perhaps even American-made greeting that he's always managed to find, wherever he's living in the world. There will be some iambic, rhyming message inside, the kind that would make us both laugh, and underneath it will be the initial of his first name, nothing more. The white space all around the message, the white space inside the card and on the back, will be full of unwritten words.

We don't write each other letters—we agreed to that, though I'm sure that he, just as I, often catches himself as he is about to begin one. There are things I wouldn't bother to write, to say to anyone else. The woods around my house are dense with thoughts untold. I don't know what we fought about so much, back then. It probably had more to do with what we didn't like about ourselves than about each other. Distance has softened all that, tricked my memory.

I slide the card out from the envelope but leave it, for the moment, face down on my lap. My hand holds it still. I look around me at the livingroom: my son's brown glazed ashtray, imperfectly round, my husband's corduroy jacket slumped across the back of a chair, the crepe paper banner trailed across the sofa. If I were dying, these are the things I would mourn for, these are the things I would miss.

But being alive and well, I think of him. I would not say he is all I need to make my life complete, because if I had him my life would be disrupted, torn apart. I would not dare to want more than this, this birthday card that comes once a year. But the idea of him, the one secret thing I carry with me, is the thing against which I measure true happiness. It is the scar beneath the sleeve that I finger in the dark.

Headlines

The highway had been built the year after I moved there, but as far as I could tell the old road was good enough. They must have expected some major immigration to our part of the state that never materialized—or else there was someone on the planning board who had a brother-in-law in construction. We had four lanes of black-as-coal roadway with bright yellow lines and nicely graded shoulders, wide enough for three cars abreast, and there were never more than one or two cars on the whole length of it at any one time. There was a practically unused cloverleaf near my house, and the southbound exit ramp took you right out onto my street. It was a huge loop of roadway which encircled what had once been a perfectly good field and a small bit of forest, and it always seemed sad to me that that piece of land should be cut off like that, forever. I wondered about animals who had gotten trapped there and were afraid to cross the asphalt. Perhaps they would go on breeding there, evolving on their own like the creatures of Galápagos.

It was still early when I got out of work, and it was one of those clear August days that made me wish I hadn't taken my vacation in July. I'd spent the morning working on the Labor Day Issue, our Back-to-School Special, which included all the predictable stuff we'd used every year for the four years I'd been at the *Dispatch*. The work was as quick as writing headlines for weddings and obits; I didn't have to read the whole article. Not like some of these news stories that are so badly written you have to read three paragraphs down before you find out what happened. The problem with a lot of the reporters on the staff is that they would rather be writing novels and their articles tend to get a bit impressionistic, the facts buried beneath a lot of dross they like to call new journalism. If the son of the town assessor breaks into Mac's ARCO and steals some parts for his pick-up truck, you don't want to have to read through a two-paragraph description of the rhododendrons along his parents' driveway before you hit the story. That's what I like about headlines; you can always get right to the facts: Service Station Robbed/Connely's Son Charged.

The little girl was sitting in the center of the field, her dress a bright spot of orange in the green. I slowed down when I noticed her, but I was already up my driveway when it struck me there was something odd about her being there, and I drove back to check it out. I had to go back on the highway and make a U-turn so I could get onto the exit ramp again. The speed limit on most highway exits is absurdly slow, and this was only 20 m.p.h., but I slowed down even more to take a better look. It was a little girl all right, wearing an orange sundress, and now she was standing in the field, watching me. I pulled off the road onto the gravel shoulder and got out of the car. She waited for me to walk up to her.

"Hello," I said, "are you here all alone?"

She was a pretty little girl—maybe five or six—with pale hair hanging down to her shoulders, bangs cut crookedly across her forehead, and bright, closely set eyes.

"Hello," she said. She didn't seem the least bit afraid of me—although children seldom are. I'm short and still wear my hair pulled back with the kind of barrettes I used when I was a kid.

"What are you doing here?" I asked.

"Just waiting."

"Whom are you waiting for?"

"Someone," she said.

I looked around. There was no one else in sight. No cars on the road. My own house was the closest building to this cloverleaf and it was invisible, beyond the trees.

"Who's that?" I asked.

"Just someone," she said, "no one special."

"Where are you from?"

"Woonsocket."

The name didn't sound like any place nearby, and, in fact, the only Woonsocket I knew was a town I had driven through, miles away, on the way to the beach.

"Woonsocket, Rhode Island?" I asked.

What We Save for Last

"It's just called Woonsocket," she said.

"Is it in the state of Rhode Island?"

"I don't know."

"Is it far from here?" I asked.

"Pretty far," she said.

"How long have you been here?"

"I don't know." She shrugged her shoulders.

She wasn't wearing a watch, and it occurred to me she was probably too young to tell time. "A long time?" I asked.

She nodded. She told me she hadn't had any lunch but that she wasn't hungry. All she wanted was a drink, she said, and she asked me if I had any lemonade at my house. It didn't strike me till afterwards that she seemed to know I lived nearby, seemed to assume I would take her home with me. At the time I was more just taken by her openness, by her directness, which seemed so unusual, even for a child. She told me her name was Monica; I had to tease her last name out of her. She pronounced it unclearly—it sounded something like "weather."

I had misgivings about taking her anywhere in my car. When I was little my mother had always warned me about getting into cars with strangers, and Monica's willingness, in fact her almost insistence on going home with me, made me uncomfortable. But I lived only five minutes away, and I thought that if I took her home and got her something to drink I could find out more about her, find out where she lived.

She liked my car because it was, in her words, "little." She liked my house, too. She ran up the steps before me and sat by the door, under the trellis that was covered with morning glories. She looked like a picture for a greeting card. A pretty little girl in a sundress, surrounded by flowers.

Inside, she ran around, looking into all the rooms. She even had me take her downstairs to show her the basement, where there wasn't much more than a washer and dryer and a huge pile of old liquor store boxes from when I had moved in, which I was saving for the next time I moved.

We made the lemonade together. She stood on the kitchen step ladder, halfway up, to stir. We sat at the kitchen table and

watched the blue jays bully the sparrows at the birdfeeder outside the window. She drank her lemonade very quickly and
finished off the cookies I put out, a whole plate-full.

"Did you have any breakfast this morning?" I asked. She
shook her head. So I made her a peanut butter and jelly sandwich and poured her another glass of lemonade, which she
finished right up.

"Now, Monica," I said, "what are we going to do with you?"

"Do you have checkers?" she asked.

"I might," I said, "but before we do anything else we have to
figure out how to get you home."

"I don't want to go home," she said. "I want to stay here with
you."

"That's terribly nice," I said, "but I am sure your Mommy and
Daddy must be terribly worried about you right now, and I
want you to help me find them."

"I don't have a Daddy," she said.

"Well, your Mommy then. Do you have a Mommy?"

"Yes," she said.

"I bet your Mommy is frantic right now, wondering where
you are."

She didn't say anything at all. She tilted her chair far back on
its two legs, so far I was sure she was going to fall over and
break her neck, but then she quickly sat up and righted it, four
legs on the floor.

"Monica, tell me, how did you get there. How did you end
up by the highway?"

"I was waiting there. And then you came and took me home
for lemonade."

"But honey, how did you get there in the first place?"

She didn't seem to understand what I was trying to find out.
"Can't we play checkers soon?" she asked.

I thought that maybe it would be easier for me to question
her, more likely she would talk, if she was distracted by a game,
so I dragged out my old checkerboard and a box of markers,
the plastic kind with ridges that make them stack so nicely. She
beat me easily, although she played with somewhat different

What We Save for Last

rules from the ones I remembered. But I didn't learn very much about her. She didn't know her address or telephone number. She couldn't spell her last name. She thought that Woonsocket was near the ocean but she wasn't sure. She seemed to have at least one brother—if Jerry was her brother—and she'd had a cat named Patsy, who had a lot of kittens, but they had all been given away and recently Patsy had been given away too. When I asked her how old she was she said "fourteen," and then she laughed and said, "No, silly, that's just a joke. Jerry taught me." But she wouldn't tell me how old she really was.

I didn't want to involve the police in the matter, at least not until I had to. Working for the *Dispatch* I knew our local station well enough, and they were capable of bungling the simplest case. I thought I would do better on my own, coaxing information out of her. And Monica seemed genuinely frightened when I brought up the subject of the police. I did call them though, just to ask if there were any reports of a missing child—newspaper training made me particularly efficient about such things—and I checked with the police in Woonsocket, Rhode Island, as well. Monica regarded me suspiciously the whole time, and when I was done she was visibly relieved.

"I'm tired," she said, "Can I take a nap?"

I thought that would be a good idea. She did look tired, and I needed some time to think about the problem, to carry out a little investigation of my own.

"Do you want to lie down on the sofa?" I asked, "or do you want to go to bed?"

She wanted to go to bed. She tried out the double bed in my bedroom, settling her head among the collection of fancy pillows that had survived much better than the marriage that had spawned them. But she opted, in the end, for the small bed in the room I used as a study and guest room.

"I like this room," she said, "It's little. Could it be mine?"

The bed was already made up. I folded up the spread.

"Let's take off your shoes," I said. I bent down and undid the buckles. They were worn-out sandals and looked too small for her. She had red marks on her feet where they had pinched. She held her arms over her head so I would help her off with her dress, too. It was a cheap dress with an elasticized top—new, but not very clean. Without the dress she looked even thinner. She had that clear skin of children, so pale you could see the tiniest veins.

"I have to go to the bathroom," she said, and she left the room. I hung her dress over the back of the chair and set her sandals neatly under it. When she came back from the bathroom she was holding her underpants in her hand. I folded them and put them on the chair with her dress. She lay flat on the bed, stretched out on the bed, stomach down. Her skin was pearly smooth without a single brown mark or blemish, except for the red ridges on the back of her ankles where her sandal straps had rubbed.

"Wait, honey," I said, "You're on top of the covers." We laughed and she scrambled off the bed so I could pull back the blanket and top sheet. Then she lay down again, face up and held up her arms so I'd tuck her in.

"Have a nice nap," I said.

"Will you kiss me good night?"

I leaned to kiss her cheek. Her skin was warm. I smoothed her bangs up off her face.

"Good night," I said.

She was asleep when I crept back in to check on her ten minutes later. She had pushed the covers off, and she was sleeping next to the wall, her little naked body pulled in close, like a diver in tuck position. I watched her sleeping there, but the curve of her shoulder, the angle of her, told me nothing more about her. She had not suffered any physical harm, none that I could see: she had not been in an accident or jumped out of a moving car. I pulled the covers over her again, and in her sleep she gripped the blanket edge and squeezed against the wall. Her only property—the dress, the underpants, the sandals—bore no clues either. The underpants were dime-store cotton, the dress bore no label, not even a size, the sandals once had writing on the inside soles but it had long since been rubbed off.

I went out to my car and got some maps and sat at the

kitchen table to study them. I pushed the plates and glasses to one side. There wasn't a single crumb on the plate where the cookies had been or on the sandwich plate. I wished I had offered Monica something more to eat. Woonsocket, Rhode Island, was more than a hundred miles away. The highway by my house did not link easily to the major roadways that were near Woonsocket—when I had passed through it was only because I had gotten off the highway, looking for a place for lunch. My town was not on the way to anyplace. There were no vacation spots around, nothing that would attract anyone unless they had friends who lived there.

I folded up the map of New England and turned to my street atlas. I looked through the list of small towns nearby. I went down the street listings looking for a Woonsocket Street, or anything that sounded like it. When Monica woke up, I decided, I would drive up and down all over the neighborhood with her, to see if we passed someplace that looked familiar. Maybe she was visiting friends or relatives in the area. Maybe her family had recently moved into town.

I called the police again. I called the police in every nearby town. There were no missing children reported anywhere at all. And by now, someone would know she was missing, wouldn't they? She'd been at my house for two hours and she had been in that field for some time before that. I tried out different scenarios in my mind. She obviously hadn't walked all the way here from Woonsocket, Rhode Island, and from the way she acted it seemed unlikely she had been kidnapped. The ease with which she had gotten into my car made me wonder if she hadn't done something like that before. She seemed so strangely comfortable with the situation, almost as if she knew what was going to happen, almost as if it had been planned this way.

I went back to my study. She was still asleep. She was lying on her back and her mouth was open. I watched her lips, but the only sound that came from them were the soft sighs of a dreaming child, no words at all.

"Monica," I said. "Monica Weather." She did not wake up.

I went back to the kitchen, saying her name over and over

again. Then I got out the telephone book. There was a Weather Phone and a Weather Forecast listing by the local radio station. There was a Weatherby and a Weatherill. I turned to the beginning of the W's and started reading out loud every name in the book. Only an inch and a half down from the Weather phone I hit it, and it all fell together with a clarity and certainty that made me catch my breath. It was as if there was a little computer in my brain, working away silently while I was doing my own work up front. When I read out the name "Weber," my computer remembered Monica's brother's name, Jerry, and then, from the files way back in my mind had retrieved a bit of information. There was an article I had done a headline for earlier that week. It had never made it into the paper, killed because the local sport shop wanted to run a larger ad, seven column inches, not three. It was a one-paragraph article saying that a group of teenagers had been picked up by the police for rowdy behavior at the drive-in and then released in the custody of their parents. One of the five, old enough not to have his name withheld, was a Jerry Weber. There was a street address, too, but I couldn't summon it. I glanced down the list of Webers, and there it was: F. Weber on Massasoit Street. The name clicked.

I went over to the phone, but then I decided to make myself a cup of tea first. Although it was more iced tea weather, I had a desire for something hot. I set the water to boil and filled my tea ball with Russian Spice tea, and while I waited for the whistle of the kettle I looked up Massasoit Street in my atlas. I expected it to be one of those small streets near me, one of those circular drives in the new development nearby. But it wasn't. It was far away, on the other side of town, across the river, past the old mills and warehouses. No child, even if she had walked all morning, could have come that far on her own.

The first cry of the kettle took me by surprise. I filled my mug and sat at the table, dunking the tea ball up and down, inhaling the aroma. I waited until the tea was cool enough to drink and then drank it slowly. I washed my cup, and I washed the two lemonade glasses and Monica's plates. The bird feeder outside had been completely emptied, and the sparrows had been left in peace to peck around on the grass for fallen seeds.

Finally I went back to the phone and called the number. A woman answered. I told her I wanted Mrs. Weber. She asked me what I wanted her for.

"I would like to discuss a matter with her involving her daughter Monica." I spoke in my newspaper voice, firm and brisk.

There was a long silence. "What about her?" asked the woman. "Who are you?"

"Are you Mrs. Weber?"

"What's this all about?" asked the woman.

"I have a little girl with me, and I'm trying to find her home," I said. "If she's your child, I'd—"

The woman cut me off. Her voice changed quickly. She had sounded rude before, now she sounded almost saccharin. "That Monica. Always wandering off. Tell me where you are, and I'll come get her."

"What relation are you to the child?"

"Relation?" said the woman. "I'm her mother."

I gave her my address and directions to my house. But I didn't feel good about it. When I hung up I looked towards the doorway and saw Monica standing there watching me.

"Put your clothes on honey," I said. "Your Mom is coming to pick you up." I tried to sound cheerful. Monica gave me no response. She seemed neither surprised nor relieved that I had tracked down her mother. She went back to the bedroom, and I followed after her and helped her on with her clothes. She didn't say one word. I thought maybe she was afraid of her mother's anger. I thought maybe she had gotten in someone's car and ended up in my part of town and was afraid of her mother finding out.

I squatted down to help buckle her sandles. "Your mother may be worried that you wandered off," I said, "but she'll be happy to see you safe and sound, I'm sure she won't be angry a bit."

"I want to stay here," said Monica. "I want to live here with you."

"I'd like that, sweetheart," I said, "that would be very nice, but you have a mother and a home. You can always come and visit me, O.K.?"

Monica turned away.

"Look," I said, "while we're waiting for your mother, why don't we play a game of checkers?"

Monica shook her head.

"Come on," I said, "I'll set them up." After a while she followed me back to the living room and reluctantly sat down and played. She didn't want to talk with me. She let me beat her three sets. We were just beginning a fourth when an old, oversized sedan came up the driveway. I stood at the window and watched while a fat woman in what might have been a waitress' uniform came up the steps to the front door.

"She put me there," said Monica. "She drove me there and told me to get out and wait until someone came."

"Till she came back for you?" I asked.

"No," said Monica, "till someone came."

"Who?"

"Just someone," said Monica.

The doorbell rang. I waited a second before reaching for the doorknob, but I didn't know what else to do, so I opened the door and let the woman in.

"I'm Mrs. Weber," she said, "thank you for calling me. I didn't know Monica even knew the number."

"She didn't," I said. "I had good luck and found you on my own."

Mrs. Weber looked puzzled, as if she were about to ask me something and then thought better of it. Then, as if remembering the purpose of her visit, she looked around until she saw Monica standing by the kitchen door.

"Well, well," she said, "I told you to play in the backyard. Wasn't this lady nice to invite you in." Monica said nothing at all, and Mrs. Weber went over to her and gave her a kind of squeeze. "Well, it's time we went home now, Monica," she said.

"Say good-bye to the nice lady and thank her for putting up with you."

"No need to thank me," I said, "I enjoyed Monica's company. I hope she'll come visit me again."

"That's very nice of you," said Mrs. Weber, "but we're moving soon."

"Well, maybe she could come over this weekend. I'd be glad to pick her up and bring her home."

"Thank you," said Mrs. Weber, "but we're moving real soon. We'll be moving the end of this week."

"Nearby?"

"Oh, no," said Mrs. Weber. "Pretty far away."

"Woonsocket?"

Mrs. Weber's face vacillated among three emotions and finally settled for the stiff smile she had been maintaining for most of our conversation.

"This little girl is full of amazing stories," she said. "Aren't you, Monica?" She looked down at her and then back at me, smiling hard. "Just a stage she's going through. Can't believe a word she says."

I wanted to snatch Monica up from her, hold Monica close against me, but something stopped me. It was Mrs. Weber's eyes. There was nothing at all about her that was the least bit like Monica—except for their eyes, which were almost identical, close-set eyes, greenish-gray with little flecks of gold in them. I knew she was no imposter but the real mother, and that I would stand no chance against her in court. Monica bore no marks of child abuse. I had no proof of anything, no proof at all.

"Say goodbye, Monica," said Mrs. Weber, who had Monica by the arm and was moving towards the door.

Monica kept her chin tucked down, her eyes fixed on her toes. Next to Mrs. Weber's bulk, she seemed even smaller and more fragile. I bent to kiss her goodbye. Mrs. Weber quickly opened the door and then reached back to pull it closed behind her. At that moment Monica turned back to look at me. There was something in her face that asked for help, but at the same time seemed resigned that it would not be forthcoming. It occurred to me, then, that perhaps this scene was not new to her, that in fact she had been tutored well, knew how to fend for herself, find food, a warm bed, a kind heart—and that if some time the person who took her home wanted her enough, as her mother hoped someone would, they would find a way to hold on to her, and never trace her back to Massasoit Street in time.

What We Save for Last

My sister Marjorie was a genius at protracting pleasure. Even when she was a little girl, she could keep a fancy lollipop untouched in its cellophane wrapper on her dresser top for weeks, and when she finally decided to eat it she would work on it over a period of days, a few licks a night. It was at Christmas that this particular talent most incurred my envy. Marjorie would space the opening of her presents to last through the whole day, starting with the packages that she suspected were unexciting (slippers or mittens) and working up to the box she guessed contained the gift she was most hoping for. I always went for the biggest box first and ripped my way through my presents as fast as I could. Then I had to spend the day hanging around my sister who still had surprises to look forward to.

Christmas morning, Marjorie and I, like most normal children, were always up before the sun. My parents had a rule that we couldn't open presents until they were up—which I remember seemed to be excruciatingly late, although I'm sure it was by seven—but we could open our stockings. My instinct was to run for my stocking and dump out the contents, but Marjorie would make me wait in the doorway while she turned on the Christmas tree lights.

"Look, Madeline," she'd say, "it's just the way Santa left it. Don't break the spell yet."

I had been set straight about Santa by some kid at school, but Marjorie persisted in supporting the myth, even though she was four years older. I thought at the time that she still believed in Santa and my parents would be angry at me if I revealed the truth to her. Now I realize that Marjorie knew the truth all along, but by protecting me from it she was able to enjoy the fantasy herself.

Marjorie was right, there was a spell cast Christmas morning: the illuminated tree in the otherwise dark living room, the boxes underneath that hadn't been there the night before, and the bulging stockings. We lived in an apartment that had no fireplace, so we hung our stockings on the knobs of the radio-victrola which was housed in an oak cabinet that always smelled, I thought, like the inside of a church. The lack of a chimney didn't faze Marjorie at all. In the city, she explained, Santa came in and out through the window. He navigated between floors of the apartment building with ropes and pulleys, like a window-washer.

I would stand in the doorway for a few minutes with Marjorie, just looking, until I couldn't stand it any longer. Then I would run for my stocking and shake its contents out on the floor. Santa invariably provided me with a chocolate reproduction of himself, and I'd quickly strip off his tinfoil garment and stuff him into my mouth in four big bites: legs, torso, arms, and head.

Marjorie would sit beside the tree with her stocking. She'd turn it slowly in her lap, examining all the bulges. Then she'd close her eyes and put her hand in, extract the first item, and try to guess its identity by touch and smell. If the first thing she hit was a tangerine or an apple, she'd eat it carefully before she went on to something else. She'd set her chocolate Santa on the bookcase, where he stood resplendent in his shiny suit in front of the untouched twelve-volume set of the Oxford Classics.

"I'll eat him after dinner," she'd tell me.

Every Christmas we got a quart of maple syrup from our cousins in Vermont, and my father always made pancakes for breakfast. He'd cook them on the griddle, two at a time, then keep them warm in the oven till he'd accumulated enough for all of us. By the time breakfast was ready I would already have opened all my presents, and, in spite of my passion for pancakes, I'd be beginning to experience the first pangs of Christmas Letdown, a syndrome that got worse as the day progressed. After breakfast my parents would sit with us by the tree and open their presents: the invariable pincushion and key case — for another rule was that we had to make their gifts ourselves. Then my mother would clean up the wreckage around the tree, salvaging the wrapping paper and ribbon that could be used another year. Marjorie's unopened presents were in a neat pile, each one destined to be opened at a particular time later in the day. I would try to goad her into opening them right away, but she was unshakeable. I was wild with curiosity about the present she had selected to be opened last, the box she would bring into our bedroom to open just before she went to sleep. One present that Marjorie opened early on was a book—we always got books for Christmas—and she'd spend most of the day curled up in the sofa reading. Sometimes, if I made a big enough pest of myself, she would set her book aside and join me in Candyland, or Parcheesi, or whatever game I had received that year. And if I was especially miserable, she would let me win.

———————

It's been more than a decade since I have seen my sister Marjorie, more than two decades since we spent a Christmas together. We write to each other occasionally and call now and then, but we live on opposite coasts of the country and neither of us has had much inclination to travel. I like to think that we are still as fond of each other as sisters can be, but the truth is that aside from our shared past, we have little in common now. Perhaps we are even afraid that if we were together, the clash of our lifestyles would jeopardize the warmth we still feel for each other.

Every Christmas, when I exchange greetings with Marjorie on the phone, I find myself talking about the Christmases when we were children. She claims she doesn't remember anything special about the way she opened presents, doesn't remember how I used to dance around taunting her to open them.

"Oh, Madeline, you're so sentimental!" she tells me now.

Perhaps I am. But this Christmas my nostalgia is inevitable because Marjorie's daughter Elaine, who is a college freshman, is spending the holiday with us. I hadn't seen Elaine since she was a little girl. Physically she resembles her father rather than her mother, but she seems to have Marjorie's streak of independence. The very spirit that made Marjorie choose a college on the far coast, then settle in California, has sent her daughter, coincidentally, back to the East Coast, the place Marjorie left behind. I thought Elaine would have wanted to fly back home this first Christmas away from her family, but she chose to stay in the area, and she doesn't seem the least bit homesick. My three children, all younger than Elaine, are delighted to have this new cousin visiting.

We've waited to set up the tree till the night Elaine joins us, when her last final exam is over. I thought decorating the tree would be a good ice-breaker, but Elaine doesn't seem to require one. She pitches right in, making replacement links for our bedraggled paper chains. When the lights and ornaments are on the tree, she joins my children tossing tinsel, the inevitable finale.

"I love this kind of tree," she tells us.

I take a quick, critical look at our tree. It's like the trees we always had when I was a child.

"What kind do you usually have?"

"Oh, you know my mother," she says, and laughs. "She has these notions. No colored lights, only the tiny clear ones. No shiny balls, just those tasteful little wooden ornaments. And no tinsel, of course."

In fact, I really don't know her mother at all anymore.

Christmas morning, my children drag Elaine downstairs with them to see Santa's bounty. Santa has left presents for Elaine, as well—Marjorie sent me her sizes—and hers, like the children's, are all open by the time breakfast makes its way to the table.

At night, after dinner, we gather around the piano and sing Christmas carols. None of us sings very well, but my husband uses a lot of pedal when he plays, and it feels very Christmasy, even though outside it has begun to rain instead of snow. After the children have been tucked in for the night, Elaine and my husband and I sit by the tree and have some eggnog. Elaine digs under the sheet that is draped around the base of the tree to resemble snow-covered hills for the paper houses, and she produces a small, wrapped box.

What We Save for Last

"It's my present from Mom," she says.

"You mean you forgot to open it all day?" my husband asks, laughing.

"Oh, no," she says, "I hid it from myself, but I knew it was there the whole time. I just like having something to look forward to opening at the end."

I knew she would say that. Just as I know what the present is as soon as she has begun to take off the paper and I see a corner of the box. It's a blue box with a surface rough-textured to resemble leather, and a gold stripe around the edge. Inside is the same string of pearls that my sister had been given for Christmas that last year she lived at home with us, the Christmas before she went away to college and never really came back. She had guessed what was in the box that Christmas, I'm sure, and it was the present she had saved for last, the present that she had brought in to bed with her to open just before she went to sleep. I had been in suspense about it all day. There was only a nightlight on in our bedroom, and in the near-darkness, from my bed across the room, I had watched her. She opened the box carefully and lifted the pearls up with both hands. She put them around her neck and closed the clasp. Then she lay back on her pillow with a moan of pleasure.

I got out of bed and tiptoed across to her.

She raised herself on her elbows and turned to me.

"I'm going to sleep with them on tonight," she told me. "But I'll let you wear them tomorrow, all right?"

"Oh, yes!" I said.

"Touch them," she whispered.

In the dark my fingers reached out towards her. I touched her warm neck and then, the pearls. I held them in my fingers. They seemed as smooth and as alive to me as her skin.

Babylove

They are the only people awake in their part of the world now, creatures on the wrong shift. Even the barred owls—there are three of them posted around the house—have ceased their calls: four interrogatives, and a descending mournful cry. This is the time when the animals who are too timid for daylight and the animals who hunt them have the earth to themselves. Shrews and mice and rabbits and foxes and strange worms that may not even have names. The earth, not large enough to accommodate all creatures at once, has devised this plan: some sleep while others live. Each territory has two distinct populations, whose lives are secret from each other.

The baby, who sleeps in a bassinet next to the mother's side of the bed, has been crying for several seconds now. In the mother's ordinary life, seconds are periods of time so insignificant they are rarely tallied, but in this new phase of her life seconds have taken on significance. Each second that the baby cries is long enough for her to have dissertations of thought. Now she debates the question "will he go back to sleep?" But her body, which, since the baby's birth, has a direct linkage to her heart, responds on its own. She sits up in bed, and her arms reach out towards the bassinet.

The baby in the bassinet, like many of the offspring of his parents' acquaintances, has been given a three-syllable name from the Old Testament. His parents have every intention to call him by it. Theirs is not a generation that takes well to nicknames. Yet the baby's name, at the moment, is theoretical only. He is The Baby, and their own names in turn, have flickered off somewhere. They are now Mommy and Daddy, and even when they speak to the baby they refer to themselves in the third person, as if they want to spare their baby, for the moment, confusion over the shared nature of the pronoun "I."

The mother thinks the baby is the most beautiful creature in the world, but in fact, as babies go, he is one of the homelier ones. He may grow up to be a man women find attractive, but now his features are indistinct behind a layer of fat, and his eyes, which are open only rarely, have a swimmy colorless quality. A red birthmark perches at the edge of one brow. It is not really disfiguring, more something that you instinctively want to brush away. The mother, who in her pregnant months tortured herself with all the possibilities of deformities known to man, is relieved by this tiny imperfection. This small blemish marks her son as human and will protect him from harm. No gods will be tempted to tamper with his perfection.

The mother hunches over the bassinet and is about to gather the baby up in her arms, but just at that second he pauses in his crying and lets out a little noise which is closer to a sigh. The father, who had begun to waken with the baby's cries and the mother's movements, seizes this reprieve and shifts back into sleep. The mother hovers, ready, by the bassinet, until she is certain the crying has really ceased, and then she climbs back into bed and settles upright, against the pillows. She is still awaiting the baby's next move. She watches the digital clock on the bureau across the room. The seconds move more quickly now, as if making up for their previous languor. The numerals are not mere bands of light, but are actual numbers on little squares that get dropped into place. She thinks of them as a miniature billboard displayed by Lilliputians—who are now working frantically to catch up.

Beside her, in bed, the father clears his throat in his sleep, as if he is about to speak, but whatever speech he has been making in his dreams he keeps to himself. The mother, who used to be an expansive dreamer, no longer dreams. She has not slept more than three hours straight since the baby was born, and when she sleeps she has no energy to waste on dreams. She turns now to watch her husband, wonders about his dreams. The baby is their first child, and both mother and father are old enough so that they thought they might never have one. She is forty, her husband is forty-two. They had been married a number of years before they began to think they were ready for parenthood, and they discovered that it was a feat not so easily accomplished. In

What We Save for Last

fact, when the baby was finally conceived it was after they each had given up hope—though they did not speak of this to each other until afterwards. The mother sees her long trial as a just punishment for what she thinks of as her ignorant selfishness for so many years. She had been afraid for her career, afraid for her marriage. She had thought of a baby as a rival for herself. Now her mistake is obvious. She had thought a baby would be Other, and the baby is, unquestionably, irrevocably, Self. Though she doesn't believe in God, she believes in some sort of divine interference. The sense of wonder that they are parents flickers in and out during her conscious hours and sustains her through all the weariness she feels. She sees herself and her husband as part of the elect.

It is quiet now in the bedroom. The baby is sleeping soundlessly; the outside world goes about its business in silence. The mother turns to watch the father's sleeping face. She is so accustomed to the baby's smallness that the father's head seems enormous, his features seem like curiosities. She has to look at his face for a long time before it recedes to its familiar proportion again.

In the evenings, before the baby was born, the father worked on a Noah's ark for him. He had started with the ark itself and then had begun making the pairs of animals, cutting them out with a jigsaw and sanding them so smooth that the pine felt like butter. He had made alligators, hippos, kangaroos, camels, and sheep and was up to the geese when the baby was born. The mother had loved the smell of the wood he worked, and she had loved watching him, his large hands forming the small figures. Now, that memory of him holds her, and as if to make it more real she reaches out and lays her palm on her husband's bare shoulder. Her palm remembers—remembers flesh, remembers something more.

She runs her fingers along her husband's shoulder, then across his chest: skin, hair, sweat—braille in the night. She nuzzles down against her husband's shoulder. She licks a small circle and then sinks her mouth down, cups his flesh in her lips. She would not actually awaken him, but she wants him to waken.

For the first time since the baby was born she forgets for a minute that she is a mother. She presses herself against her husband's side. He is still asleep, but his free arm moves up, and he reaches for her across his chest. She takes his hand and lays it on her breast.

"Touch me," she asks him softly. "Please touch me."

His hands rests for a minute on her body, but then he moves his shoulder and his hand drops down against his hip. He coughs once and his mouth stays half-open, his lips moving slightly with his breath.

The mother leans back against the pillows. Her breasts have filled up, and they are so hard they feel like wood. She gets up slowly and leans over the bassinet. The baby is sleeping still. She touches the side of his cheek. Milk starts streaming down from both breasts. She scoops the sleeping baby up in her arms and gets back into bed. She braces her elbow against her husband's side and lifts the baby up in place. Even in his sleep he turns his face toward her breast. She pushes her nipple into the baby's parted mouth.

"Suck, darling," she whispers. "Suck. Suck."

Downstream

I'd misjudged two things: the current in the river, and my brother Gilbert. It had been a dry summer and the river was low, the current slower than I'd ever known it. As for Gilbert—well, my mother complained that he was lazy, sulky, and sarcastic, but complaining has always been one of her specialties. I hadn't spent much time with Gilbert since he'd turned from boy into teenager, not since I'd gone away to college six years before. On this visit to my parents' I'd dreamed up the idea of taking Gilbert on a canoe trip, to make things up to him a little. It was something I hadn't done in years, not since my brother John and I were both living at home.

We'd parked my car downstream at Tucker's Landing, and a friend had driven us and our canoe upstream to the public access area just south of Haydn Falls. I figured that stretch would take us a few hours, but the river, which I thought I knew, was a different creature from the one I had remembered. When we got the canoe into the water we had to pole our way out through weeds and muck to get to a channel.

"What kind of a river is this anyway?" asked Gilbert. "You could walk right across!"

"It's usually deeper than this," I said.

"I'm hungry," said Gil. "When do we eat?"

"We paddle a bit first," I said. "Then we keep our eye out for a nice place to stop."

"You said there were islands."

"There are islands," I said, and passed him the map of river, our route marked in red pencil. Gil consulted it, paddle dragging.

"Hey, this looks like it will take us all day! There's something I want to watch on TV at five."

"We'll be back by five."

Gilbert, my parents' mistake, or, as they called him, their "surprise," was born more than a decade after my brother John and me. They'd had one of each, a girl and a boy, and then they had this third child, this odd man out, who upset the symmetry. But he was still the darling, most beloved, most beautiful baby boy, born to entertain my mother and distract her from the possibility of ever returning to her career, and to keep my father well enough supplied with bills so he could never think about retirement. The darling baby was now a thirteen-year-old conundrum. My mother scolded and wept in rapid alternation. My father reassured her that he'd grow out of it, but he constantly lost his temper and issued idle threats. Gilbert, an only child now in the big house, retreated to his room—my old room—where he drew endless pictures of sailboats. This boy who lived a hundred miles from any ocean and had never been on a sailboat in his life. Sailing was now his great passion, that and the gerbils, whom he lavished with affection and watched for hours.

"I'm hungry," said Gilbert. He looked at his watch. He had one of those digital watches equipped with a stop watch, an alarm, and games, all of which worked at ocean depths, in case you had a desire to play Space Invaders 10,000 feet under the sea. "It's 12:48," he wailed. "I knew I had a right to be hungry."

"OK, Gil," I said. I was surprised to realize it was that late, although the sun was straight overhead and I should have known. Everything had taken much longer than I had expected: finding the paddles in the back of my parents' garage, packing the picnic lunch, getting the canoe on the car, and finally, tearing Gilbert away from the Saturday morning cartoons. Sylvester the cat, who had suffered some mortal injury, and sported little wings, was chasing some anonymous four-legged creatures around the clouds.

I took in my paddle and reached for the lunch basket. "Let's just eat as we drift along."

Gil grumbled, but he made himself an easy chair out of the life preserver pillows. I passed him a sandwich and a cup of lemonade, and he seemed content there, sprawled with his long, skinny legs up over the sides of the boat, his big feet rippling the water.

Gil had grown about two inches since I'd seen him at Easter

What We Save for Last

time. Every holiday I was at my parents' he was taller and skinnier, as if he had been stretched on a rack the whole time I was away. Even his face, once round and cherubic, had a pinched look, and his nose seemed long and thin. Only his eyes, gray-green, with long black lashes, were still beautiful. They were obviously waiting for his body to fill out and grow handsome again.

The river was almost canal straight at this point. There were spindly trees on both sides of the high banks. I knew that up beyond them, out of view, corn and tobacco fields stretched across the valley. I heard a tractor in the distance and spotted a cloud of brown dust, and then, as it angled away, a man on the tractor. I thought about him working his fields in the heat and seeing us, lazing down the river. I let us coast for a minute and trailed my finger in the water, thinking of how, at the end of the day, the farmer would throw off his clothes and plunge into the river, and how cool the water would feel against his skin.

We coasted slowly down the river and the current turned us broadside. I copied Gil and settled low in the canoe, and we both looked over the side. The sun made the surface a solid black, a mirror for the sky, but shadows broke the sun's glaze and revealed the river below, the weeds like long hair, all flowing south, the river bottom studded with slender pink clam shells.

"There's a catfish!" I called out.

"I don't see him."

"They look like fat gray rocks, about a foot long, but you can tell them by their whiskers."

"I never see anything," Gil whined, but after a while he saw one, then another, then a school of smaller fish that fanned out around our boat.

"How was your week on that camping trip?"

"O.K."

"Did you sleep out in tents?"

"Of course, what did you think we slept in?"

"Did you see any wildlife?"

"Nothing interesting. Just a lot of chipmunks and a skunk.

No bears or anything. The kids who went up there last year saw a bear. He got into their garbage."

"That happened to us, once, when I was a kid," I said. "We rented a cabin somewhere and during the night a bear got into the garbage. Dad went out with the flashlight and he said the bear took one look at him and he took one look at the bear, and they were both frightened and took off."

"I've heard that story from Dad a hundred times."

"Sorry," I said, "I didn't know."

I got back on my seat and picked up my paddle. The wide, straight course of the river had come to an end, but the river was as sluggish as before. When I consulted the map I realized that we had done only about an eighth of the trip and regretted my leisurely lunch.

"Gil," I said, "The river's a lot slower than I thought. You'll have to pitch in and do a little paddling."

"It's too hot," said Gil. "I want to go for a swim."

"We'll swim when we get to the islands," I said. Gil moaned and sat up and took a few strokes in the water.

"I don't like this paddle," he said, "the metal gets my hands all black."

"Want to use mine?"

"Yup. You took the nicer one."

I exchanged paddles with Gil.

"My shoulder's all achy," he said, a few minutes later.

"Time to change sides."

"I can't do it," said Gil, "it's all backwards."

"Like this," I said.

Gil imitated a few strokes, then bashed his thumb into the side of the boat. He spent the next two miles nursing his thumb, complaining about the design of canoes, and extolling the virtues of sailboats. I just kept paddling. On a sandbar in the river I spotted a Snowy Egret, the "Golden Slipper" bird, with its dark legs and yellow feet. Its feathers were unbelievably white, the stuff of clouds. Gilbert was impatient when I stopped paddling and trained my field glasses on him.

"It's just a dumb bird," he said.

It was late afternoon when we got to the string of islands I had hoped to reach by lunchtime. The water level was so low that uncharted islands dotted the river, some thin ridges of rocks, some just strips of sand. We stopped at the first one that had vegetation and pulled the boat up onto the pebbled shore. I walked across to the sandy side of the narrow island and waded out.

"We have time for only a quickie," I said. I plunged into the water and floated on my back. Gil followed me reluctantly. "It's too cold," he said.

"It's wonderful," I said. I swam out a bit but suddenly felt myself caught in a swift current. I struggled to get back where I could dig in with my feet.

"The current's bad here," I called out to Gil. "Don't come out this far."

Gil gave me a dismissive look, ran into the river, and swam out as far as I was. Fortunately he was upstream of me.

"Nancy, help!" he screamed as the current caught him. I grabbed onto him just as he swept past me. We got back to shore and lay down on the sand next to each other till we caught our breath. For a moment the arrogance was completely washed from his face, changing his features back into the soft look he'd had as a boy.

"That was something," said Gil. "All we have to do is ride in that current now. We'll be at Tucker's Landing in five minutes flat."

"The river widens downstream. I'm afraid it will be slow going again."

Unfortunately I was right. Not far south of the islands we were back to our sluggish pace, and we still had quite a few miles ahead of us. The sun, which had been so bright and seemed so fixed in place when we started, was edging down now, settling toward the west. Now and then it was a victim of the clouds which crossed the sky.

"Gil," I said, "I'm afraid I misjudged things a bit. We have farther to go than I'd thought. You'll have to paddle, too. We'll never get there if I have to do it all myself."

Gil took a few furious strokes, then sat back panting.

"I'm tired."

"At least don't drag your paddle in the water."

"I didn't even want to come on this dumb trip," said Gil. "It was all your idea."

"It was my idea. But when we talked about it yesterday you were excited. I didn't force you to come. We're in this together, and if you pulled your own weight things would be a lot better."

"Well, I think the whole thing was a dumb idea," said Gil. He picked up his paddle and did some symbolic strokes.

The shoreline along the way changed with agonizing slowness. I kept picking out little markers for myself—a fisherman along the bank, an irrigation pump, high tension wires strung across. I'd work hard to reach them, then let myself catch my breath. I'd never paddled so long and so hard before in my life.

South of the railroad bridge the river was joined by a smaller one. From this point south it was deep enough for motorboats. The current picked up, so we moved along faster, but the river was more treacherous. Teenagers in high-powered boats, boys showing off for their dates, set up patterns of waves that almost swamped us. Boats pulling water skiers veered dangerously close. I thought we'd be safer closer to shore, but I was worried about fallen trees in the river. Along a stretch of beach I saw the body of a white bird that had washed up on shore. It looked like something had broken its neck.

While I worked to steady the canoe after one encounter, Gil waved at the boat.

"Did you see that super turbo? I wish we had a boat like that instead of this dinky canoe."

"A boat like that couldn't go farther up the river where we were."

"So who'd want to?"

"Gil, why must you be this way?"

"What way?"

"Argumentative, disagreeable—"

"Why? what did I say?"

What We Save for Last

"It's not just what you say. It's your tone. You're impatient, you're surly. People won't want to talk with you."

"So don't talk with me."

I went back to paddling. I had to keep steering us towards shore to keep from being swamped. One Crisscraft circled us twice and it was all I could do to keep us steady. The kids on the boat waved and shouted and held their beer bottles in the air. I remembered that it was a Saturday night and that probably a lot of them were already drunk.

"You promised we'd be home by five," whined Gil. "I had a show I wanted to watch."

"I'm doing the best I can, Gil," I said.

"Why can't we just go ashore here?"

"Because our car's down at Tucker's Landing. We'd have no way to get home."

I'd been paddling mostly on my right side, my stroke on the left wasn't very good, but now my shoulder hurt so much I tried one side, then the other. The sun, which had been white-yellow overhead, was getting redder. By the time we rounded the next bend in the river it had sunk down another notch and was grazed on the bottom rim by the distant trees.

"Please, Gil," I asked. "Can't you do a little paddling?"

"Why'd you get us into this?"

"I didn't know it would be this way. For God's sake, Gil, do things always work out the way you expect them to, do you make all the right decisions all the time?"

Gil, his back to me, was paddling with small, dainty strokes. "Do you?"

"You don't have to shout at me." He turned around now.

"What do I have to do? What do I have to do to let you know that we're in a dangerous situation, and we may not get out of it without your help."

"What's the big worry?" asked Gil. "What are you all uptight about?"

"I'm worried about being out on the river after the sun has set. We don't even have a flashlight. We won't be able to see where we're going. And the drunken motorboat drivers won't be able to see us in the dark, either."

I gazed up, then down the river. For the moment, boats coming upstream could see us clearly, silhouetted against the hot red sky, but boats coming downstream would have a hard time. Our canoe was dark green, our clothes and towels were dark colors, too.

"You should always carry a flashlight with you," said Gil. "It's one of the first rules of sailing."

"Thanks a lot, Gil, I'll remember that."

As we came around a bend, a line of spindly, nearly leafless tress along the bank stood out like barbed wire in front of the sunset. I felt like running up to the ridge and holding on to the edge of the sun to keep it from sinking out of sight. I thought of primitive humans, worried that they might never see the sun again.

When the sun was gone, irrevocably, all that was left was a faint blush in the sky, and, for a very short while, a kind of soft, shimmery light. Then it got dark.

"Please Gil," I said. "you've got to help out now."

Gil didn't answer. He looked over to where the sun had vanished and put his paddle back in the water. The surface of the water was black, no longer a window to its depths. The sun had taken that, too. The banks were dark tangles of vine-covered trees, some which had lost their footing and toppled into the water. I thought about taking the risk and just pulling up on shore, but the banks were too steep, the shoreline too uncertain. The barking of dogs in the distance reminded me that these were sheep-grazing fields and we'd run the dangers of guard dogs and electric fences.

"I'm cold," said Gil, in a small voice. "Aren't we almost there?"

"I don't think we have too far to go."

"Are you sure?"

"No, I'm not sure."

"Aren't you sure about anything?"

"No, I wish I could be."

"Why'd you take me on this dumb trip anyway?"

"Because I thought it would be nice to spend some time together."

"You don't come home very much anymore."

"I can't get back East that often. You know I have a job and—"

"You and John left all your old stuff behind, but you never spend any time home. You don't know what it's like being the only one left there. I have to listen to Mom nagging me all the time. I have to listen to Mom and Dad fighting all the time. Someday they'll get divorced, just like everybody else's folks."

"I don't think so, Gil—"

"I don't care, it's just that I wish I could move away from home like you and John."

"You will. You'll be going to college, and then you'll be off on your own. When you're my age—"

I heard the sound of a motorboat approaching around the bend.

"It doesn't have any lights!" cried out Gil.

"I'm heading us in to shore," I said. "I'd rather risk trees in the water."

But there wasn't time to get out of the channel, and I didn't want us to get hit broadside. I quickly turned us so we were heading back downstream.

"Sit down in the bottom, Gil," I shouted, "hold on to the sides."

The motorboat zoomed past us so close, we were showered by its spray. The water was cold. We rocked wildly back and forth in the wake.

"Keep down, Gil!" I screamed. I heard the motorboat circle around up river. It came past us again. I closed my eyes and held on tight. The waves sloshed over the sides of the canoe. My knees stung.

I opened my eyes when I heard the motorboat recede in the distance. The waves began to dissipate and the canoe's rocking became rhythmic, then slowed.

"O.K., Gil," I said. "We better get paddling. Not too fast, just steady. We've got to get out of here before another boat comes along."

"I'm paddling," said Gil.

Everything looked the same. Only the sound of the water against the boat gave me the sensation we were really moving; otherwise it looked as if we were just paddling nowhere, in place. Everything hurt me: my knees, my shoulder, my back, but the pain and fatigue and cold were almost reassuring reminders, something tangible to keep my fear from taking over. In the far distance I could hear the sound of a motorboat.

"Lights!" called out Gil. "I think I see some lights."

I looked hard. The lights seemed steady, like something on land, rather than on a moving boat.

I kept paddling long after I thought I couldn't take another stroke, and slowly the lights became clear.

"I think that's Tucker's Landing," I said. "It has to be."

The lights ran along the dock at the landing. I knew where there was a concrete boat ramp, and I headed for that.

"Pull your paddle in, Gil, and get ready to jump out," I said.

As soon as we touched, Gil leaped out, then slipped back into the water.

I got out, slipped too, but we were able to pull the boat up on ground. Gil was wet and shivering.

"I've got a blanket in the car," I said. "Let's warm up first, then worry about the boat later."

We ran up to the parking lot, where ours was the only car, and I found the blanket in the trunk. I wrapped it around Gil's shoulder, then mine, and pulled him close. He sobbed against my chest.

"It's all right, honey," I said. "We made it."

"I miss you, Nancy," he cried. "I miss you. I'm the only one who's left home now. We're never going to be a family again. You come home less and less every year and soon you'll never come home at all."

"Of course I'll always come home," I said. "And we'll always be a family, no matter what."

The gravel of the parking lot felt wonderfully firm beneath my feet. The future seemed both certain and bountiful. I thought: someday Gil and I will be old, and he'll be a father telling his teenage son about this canoe trip, and his son will remind him he's told the tale a hundred times before.

Small Sins

It was the sin of a second, a very small sin, yet over the years the scene comes back to Alice with a clarity and consistency that few of her childhood memories have. Now, as she stands in the kitchen making tea, she hears her mother's voice coming from the new wing behind the pantry, and the scene replays itself once more. Flocked wallpaper — black velvet latticework on gold — superimposes itself over the kitchen cabinets, and a Kirman carpet covers the quarry tile beneath her feet.

Alice had been eight then, her brother, Jeremy, ten. The doorbell was ringing with uncharacteristic insistence. When her mother finally answered it, the elevator man burst in with his message: Jeremy had been hit by a car in front of their apartment building. The police, he said, were already there; an ambulance was on its way. Alice, forgotten in the commotion, had squeezed back against the wall. Her mother cried, "Oh my God!," looked wildly around the foyer, snatched her fur coat from the chair, and ran for the door. But just before she left, she caught a glimpse of herself in the mirror over the hall table. The face that confronted her was her morning face, the face of a woman who slept late and had not yet put on her makeup or done her hair. She hesitated, then she took a few seconds to find a lipstick in her pocketbook on the table and to smear some color on her lips.

"Where's my watch?" Alice hears her mother call out now to her nurse. "I'm sure I left it right here, on the nightstand."

"I don't see it, Mrs. Singer." The nurse's voice is emotionless, neither impatient nor patient. "Why don't we have some breakfast now and I'll find it for you later."

Alice takes the tea bag from her mug and drops it into the sink. She usually adds milk to her tea, but she wants to be out of the kitchen before her mother comes in. She wants to avoid an encounter until lunchtime, if she can.

In her study at the far end of the house, even with her door shut, Alice can hear her mother's voice, though she can't make out the words. Alice's mother still speaks as if she's on stage. She's quite given up, as she puts it, on Alice's voice, but whenever she has the opportunity she instructs Alice's children to speak from their diaphragms.

At the height of her career as an actress, Alice's mother had a minor part in a long-running soap opera. Alice's father believed in his wife's talent and beauty. He was grateful to her for taking time out to bear him two children. He put all his energies into earning money for her and asked little of her in return. He was content that his children be raised by a succession of nursemaids whose English was only marginal, then dispatched to boarding school. He had died of a heart attack when he was forty-eight, while Alice and Jeremy were away at school and his wife was on a cruise. He'd left her a wealthy widow, probably not minding death so much as long as he knew she was well provided for.

It is impossible for Alice to do anything that requires real thought this morning. All she can do is custodial work — go through her mail, make back-up copies of some computer disks, file photocopies of some research material. She tries to close out the distant voice, but she strains to listen all the same. Her daughter has lent her a portable tape recorder with a tape of Vivaldi, but Alice has found she can't work with background music either. What she longs for is silence. After all those years of craving quiet time while her children were small, now they are in school all day and she still has no peace. It is not even her mother's voice, but the idea of her voice. The only pure quiet time Alice has is when her mother naps, but it is like the time when her children were babies and those brief interludes while they napped were so precious, so precarious, she couldn't relax enough to use them well.

"But, honey, what did you think it would be like?" Charlie, her husband, had asked her.

Alice takes a sip of tea and holds the warm mug against her cheek. She closes her eyes. Her mother was leaning in towards the mirror, her chin thrust out. The gold lipstick case gleamed

What We Save for Last

in her hand. How old was she then? Forty? Forty-five? The age
Alice is now. Her mother's coat was a dark brown fur — mink
probably — and Alice remembers how she liked to part the
longer, stiffer hairs and nuzzle in the soft underfur. Her mother
said it ruined the fur, so Alice did it when she wasn't looking.
The coat had a shawl collar and a few strands of her mother's
blond hair were always there. Alice's hair is brown, was brown
as a child, as was Jeremy's, one of her mother's grievances. Her
mother's hair was not naturally blond, and she would probably
have been more attractive with dark hair, but she felt blondness
was superior. She had a way of saying "blond" as if it were not
merely a hair color but a character trait. Even now, an old
woman with a body that has long since relinquished any claim
to beauty, she still has her hair colored regularly and worries
about her roots growing out, even though they are no longer
brown but white.

It is Jeremy who should be disturbed by the scene, Jeremy
who lay injured while his mother stood by the mirror upstairs,
lipstick in hand. But at the time, of course, Jeremy knew nothing, and years later, when Alice told him about it, he shrugged
it off. He had no illusions about their mother; he wouldn't let
himself be hurt by her. He had survived the incident with a
broken leg and stitches. He had survived his childhood. Now he
lives on the far coast of the country, sends his mother flowers
on Mother's Day and thinks about her as infrequently as possible. When he'd heard she couldn't continue living alone in her
apartment in New York, he thought a nursing home was the
only solution. He told Alice she was crazy to take her in.

Outside Alice's study window, the squirrels are hard at work
devising ways to plunder the birdfeeder. Alice and they have
been at war for years, and there is no squirrel baffle they haven't
eventually outsmarted. Alice has recently installed a metal dish
that frustrates them when they shinny up the pole, and she
moved the feeder so it's a long jump from the nearest tree, but
one little red squirrel, who is even more agile than the grays,
keeps trying. So far he has succeeded only in disrupting the
mourning doves who waddle around the base of the feeder,

pecking at the sunflower seeds scattered by the blue jays. Alice is torn between rapping on the window to chase this squirrel away and rooting for him for his dexterity and perseverance. It is difficult to know if the squirrel is motivated by true hunger or by greed. It's February, and although the acorn supply seemed abundant this year, you can't be sure. Alice does rap on the window, but she's glad the squirrel ignores her. Alice's mother thinks she should take the feeder down altogether and keep the squirrels away from the house. She sees them simply as rodents and is convinced they carry rabies. It amuses Alice to contrast her mother with the kind of old ladies who spend their golden years feeding squirrels in Central Park. As she has gotten older, Alice's mother has taken an even sharper dislike to small animals, all animals in fact. She complains that the family dog keeps her awake with his barking, the hamsters carry germs, and Alice's daughter's horse encourages flies. Alice has not told her about the current invasion of field mice in the house, has not told her that every morning, before Charlie leaves for work, he makes his rounds emptying and resetting traps in the basement. Fortunately Alice's mother's eyesight has deteriorated with the rest of her body. If she saw a mouse in the kitchen—a place they frequent with regularity—she would probably make a scene and insist on being brought back to New York.

And she can't live in New York alone. She can afford a full-time nurse, can afford anything she wants, but it is impossible to hire someone responsible around the clock to care for her there. Impossible to find someone whom she will tolerate, who can put up with her for any length of time. They'd gone through a succession of nurses. Alice's mother claimed they cheated her, robbed her, and neglected her. In the end each had walked out on her. Alice had to drive four hours down to the city every few days for each crisis in her mother's life, a life where crisis had become a habit. Her mother refused to go into a nursing home; instead she had built a wing onto Alice's house, a little apartment, with its own sitting room, bathroom, and two bedrooms.

There is a modest tapping at Alice's study door, and she knows it is the nurse, bringing a summons from her mother. Alice gets up and opens the door.

"Can it wait?" she asks.

"That's not for me to say," says the nurse.

Alice wants to share a smile with her, but the nurse has been conscientiously professional and Alice is so grateful to have found someone who will stay with her mother that she is afraid to do anything to upset the balance. Alice can't tell if this woman's calm, flat manner is characteristic of her personality or an attitude she assumes for her job, just as she can't tell whether the nurse really believes her mother was a famous actress and is interested in the scrapbooks and narratives she provides or feels it is her professional duty to listen, never flattering, never diminishing.

"Tell her I'll be there in a few minutes."

When she goes in to her mother, it is fifteen minutes later. She had simply sat at her desk, drawing doodles in the margins of her yellow pad of paper, angry at her mother for causing her to exact this small, fruitless vengeance.

"There you are, at last," says her mother. She is sitting at the table that doubles as her desk, and spread before her is an array of papers and manila folders. She has taken to wearing velour jogging suits; when she found a style she liked in a catalogue she ordered it in all available colors. This morning's is magenta.

"Is there something you need?" Alice asks. She remains standing, even though her mother taps on the seat of the chair next to her. Her mother looks up at the nurse.

"Why don't you go to the drugstore now that Alice is finally here," she says. "And take the empty bottle with you so they can't make a mistake this time. It's the cream I want, not the lotion, and if they don't have it, they should order it for me."

Alice's mother waits until the nurse has not only left the house but is actually backing out the driveway before she speaks.

"Sit down, Alice," she says, "There are some financial matters I have to go over with you."

"I'm sorry, Mother, but I can't right now. Mornings are my worktime. We agreed on that. I'll spend time with you this afternoon."

"Alice, there are some things of considerable importance here that we need to discuss, and there are some papers I need you to sign."

"They can wait till after lunch. They aren't going to disappear before then."

Alice's mother removes her reading glasses from her face and turns to her sharply. "It's about time, Alice, that you developed some sense about this business. I'm not going to be around that long, you know, to manage everything for you."

"How can you say something like that? You don't manage anything for me; all you do is fuss with your own investments, sending your poor lawyer and accountant on endless errands." Alice takes in her breath slowly. "Look, Mother, I don't want to get into an argument about this with you. I want to get back to work. You don't understand I have a job to do, a life to lead. I need my mornings. You just can't keep interrupting me time after time."

"If you don't want me living here, Alice, just say so. I have a perfectly lovely apartment sitting there in New York."

Alice turns slowly and walks through the house to her study. She doesn't close the door, but she sits at her desk with her back to the doorway. Although her mother has to use an aluminum walker, she follows Alice with impressive speed and stands in the doorway.

"I'm not going to put up with this from you," says Alice's mother. "I expect better treatment from those who claim to love me."

Alice waits a long time before she turns to face her mother. "I don't love you," she says.

"You do love me," shouts Alice's mother as she pounds her walker on the floor. "You do, you do." Then she stomps back to her own room.

Alice turns on her computer and puts in a disk. The hum of the fan in the disk drive is comfortingly familiar. When the opening message appears on the screen, she dutifully types in the date, but she can't decide which function to select: Create, Edit, or Print a document. She stares at the choices.

Was it a sin, then, to not love your own mother? Or was the sin in saying so?

Alice presses the letter "C" for create a document, and the computer monitor offers a new, blank screen.

"Dear Jeremy," Alice types. "In your last letter you wondered how much longer I thought we could keep this arrangement going. The doctor told me this week that Mother could 'linger' this way for months, possibly years. It seems to be a favorite word of his. I've decided that I will stick it out with her here until the end, and Charlie, dear soul, is willing, if it's what I want. Though he, like you, thinks it's nuts. You know, I'm sure, I'm doing it for myself, not for her. (In one of our more awful scenes, just now in fact, she bullied me into admitting I didn't love her.) It's not masochism at all. It's that I don't want to ever have anything to feel guilty about. I don't want her to ever have that kind of power over me."

Alice hears a car coming up the driveway, undoubtedly the nurse back from town. The car door slams, then the kitchen door. Not long afterwards she hears her mother's voice:

"What do you mean they wouldn't order, of course they'll order it. Didn't you tell them who I am?"

Alice looks out the window. The red squirrel is perched alertly on the bird feeder, gorging himself on sunflower seeds. He is perfectly frozen there, except for the working of his miniature hands and jaws.

Alice turns back to her monitor. She reads over what she has written. Then she pushes the delete key on the keyboard, and she erases the words on her screen. One by one, the letters tumble off into oblivion, fall from grace.

Margaret, Are You Grieving?

Spring and Fall
— to a young child

Margaret, are you grieving
Over Goldengrove unleaving?
Leaves, like the things of man, you
With your fresh thoughts care for, can you?
Ah! as the heart grows older
It will come to such sights colder
By and by, nor spare a sigh
Though worlds of wanwood leafmeal lie;
And yet you will weep and know why.
Now no matter, child, the name:
Sorrow's springs are the same.
Nor mouth had, no nor mind expressed
What heart heard of, ghost guessed:
It is the blight man was born for,
It is Margaret you mourn for.

Gerard Manley Hopkins

There are no shells to gather, but the sand is as pink as
the tourist guides had promised. The entire island has
been designed to look happy. Houses are painted the
colors of Easter Eggs—pink with green shutters, green with
blue shutters, purple with white shutters, yellow with orange
shutters. And there are flowers everywhere—not confined to the
gardens, but overflowing from bushes and trees and vines—and
flowers at eye level, above your head, and at your feet.

The sand, as Margaret bends to examine it, is not really pink
at all, nor is it really sand. It is made up of tiny bits of shells
and coral, some white, some cream, some bubble-gum pink,
specks of color, that blend to form one color, like when you

step back from a pointillist painting. A darker band, where the shells are more coarsely ground, marks the tide's farthest reach. Margaret follows along this ridge, her head low, eyes adjusting to the smallness. She picks out miniature shells that are perfectly intact—limpits and clams and scallops, tiny as birdseed—little parts of calcified plants, white twigs, and pink twigs, some like miniature hands, some like teeth. It is a pretty graveyard, this beach, and once her eye gets used to the scale, it is as interesting to her as the bay beaches on Cape Cod, where as a child she would go and gather what seemed like a sampling of everything that had ever lived in the entire ocean world.

Far back along the beach Margaret's husband, Victor, is reading the local newspaper, reading, he claims, to learn something about the culture—the price of houses, the scores of the cricket matches, the foreign comics. He looks up now and then and squints in her direction—checking on her the way parents check on a child's wanderings. She does not mind. She is not sure of anything she does, not even the footsteps she leaves in the sand, and she is grateful that Victor is here to look after her. If she is to survive—though she has not so much chosen to as resigned herself to it—she will do so because of Victor's care. And to the best of her ability, she tries to help Victor keep her safe. She stays away from the edges of cliffs, those beautiful promontories where people look out and see the sweep of the island. She stays away from cliffs because she is afraid she will throw herself to the wind, not so much seeking death, as lusting for the fall itself, the comfort of that short space of air. On the motorbike, tight behind Victor, she hooks her hand under his belt so she will not let go, as she is tempted to, and throw her arms up and let herself go flying off behind him.

Victor is kind to her, kind and gentle, and generous. And although she has no fear that the kindness will ever stop—for Victor, she believes, will stick by anything he has ever loved—she fears that the sincerity of the kindness, the inclination, the love, cannot last. She fears that the part of him that is more man than saint will assert itself soon—resentful, bitter. She feels she is living on borrowed time. At some point she will have to give up grieving and be as she was—or Victor's life cannot go on—but now she cannot imagine how that will ever come to be. Her grief over Jeanie seems to her even greater than her love for Jeanie—and that love was, she had imagined, infinite.

She has strayed far down the beach, and Victor is standing now, calling to her. He is too far away for her to see the concern on his face, but his voice carries, "Margaret, are you—?" She hears her name, hears the beginning of the question "Margaret, are you all right?" She waves to show him that she is and starts back in his direction. "Margaret, are you—?" Then, suddenly, she remembers the first line of a poem she has not thought of in years. *Margaret, are you grieving?*

She would have been struck by that poem even if her name had not been Margaret. She was a freshman in college, and poetry was something new for her. She had thought the poem was about a girl feeling sad about the end of autumn, about time passing, about growing old, but her English teacher had given her a failing grade on her paper. The poem, he insisted, was about the Fall of Man. Even now, thinking back twenty years, she is angry at him. She is still an ardent atheist. Autumn, time, mortality were the real stuff, the Catholic theory of the Fall of Man was not.

Margaret, are you grieving?

Yes, she, Margaret, is little else. She has become her grief; it is all she is. It has wiped out everything else she has ever been, as thoroughly as the waves that wipe away the ridges of sand they have deposited before, as the sound of the waves wipes away Victor's voice in the distance, calling her, calling to see if she is safe.

A Long-tail, the extravagance of his tail sweeping out behind him, an improvement on a gull's grace, glides low over the waves and then up and away. Margaret stands still. The poem's last line comes to her as clearly as if someone else, not just a voice in her mind, is reciting it: *It is Margaret you mourn for.*

It *is* Margaret she mourns for—mourns because Jeanie was mortal, and because she, Jeanie's mother, though mortal too, was doomed to outlive Jeanie. To steady herself, Margaret looks down at the sand, looks back at the trail of footprints she has left—but she is betrayed. She imagines Jeanie's small footprints in the sand, and although she struggles to push Jeanie out of her mind, she cannot avoid those footprints, cannot stop picturing how they would mark the sand next to her own. She crouches down. There is something lurking in her mind, something even worse than the simple recital of facts. It is remote and complex and terrible, yet her mind recklessly seeks it out.

The day before it had rained, and they had gone into town by bus to shop. In the afternoon, when it cleared, they took the small ferry back across the bay to their part of the island. At the landing there was a pink playhouse-sized waiting room with a white sugar-cube roof and fresh white steps leading up the hillside to the street. They stopped halfway up to catch their breath and to get a view of the bay.

"Let me take that," said Victor, relieving Margaret of one of the pink and green plastic shopping bags she was carrying, adding it to his two. The bags were filled with sweaters, which were supposed to be the island's great bargain, and Margaret had done her best to be interested in them. She was indifferent to sweaters, as she was indifferent to everything, and she knew that Victor would buy her anything she wanted, yet she had entered the game of choosing. She had matched the blue with the cable stitch against the yellow with the yoke collar, the cashmere against the lambswool. You could fill a life with such things.

They followed the guidebook and took an old Tribe Road—one restricted to pedestrians—back to their hotel. The walls on either side of the path were high as their heads, and vines and branches reached across, blocking out the sun. Victor used his rolled-up umbrella to clear the cobwebs before them. The spiders were the largest Margaret had ever seen, black, with bushy legs. She planned to look them up when they got home. The insect book—she had often looked at it with Jeanie—was

　　　　　　　　　　　　　　　　　What We Save for Last

one of the few books associated with Jeanie that had not been packed away.

The spider webs ended at the top of the hill where the Tribe Road leveled off. The walls on either side were low enough there for Margaret to look over at the fields of squat banana trees. On one side there was a stately house painted lime green with white shutters. The shutters were hinged at the top of the windows and propped open at the bottom, giving the house—Margaret always thought of windows as eyes—a vaguely oriental look. At the end of the fields, the Tribe Road took a sudden turn and the jungle seemed to close in on them again. Just as they stopped to consult the map, they heard the approaching sound of a galloping horse. Instinctively they both jumped back and pressed against the underbrush.

The horse that charged out from nowhere was larger than life, a black horse ridden by a dark-skinned man, barechested and barefoot, with hair corded to his waist. The man pulled the horse up short and turned to look at them—at her, Margaret, clutching her pink and green shopping bag. The man was riding bareback, but the bridle was decorated with silver medallions. The horse reared and shrieked, his nostrils flared wide as the nostrils of a carousel horse. When Margaret opened her eyes a second later, the horse was gone from sight, and the sound and the dust had settled so quickly it looked as if it had never been disturbed. The smell of oleander rose above the smell of the road.

"I think he was a Rastafarian," said Victor.

"Here?"

"They must get around." Victor set his bags down, and put his arms around her. "Hey?" he asked gently. "Were you afraid? I thought you were just surprised."

She held her cheek hard against his chest. "Some of both," she said. And there was a flicker of joy—so brief she almost didn't recognize it before it was gone. Joy to have been so frightened? Joy to have escaped? Joy to have wanted to survive?

"I thought you were the old horsewoman," said Victor.

"No, no," she laughed. "I haven't ridden for years. And I was never very good."

"I thought you were going to show me up tomorrow," said Victor, "leave me behind on my old nag."

"We're both going on old nags," she said, "if you please."

This had been her one suggestion for their vacation. Looking through brochures about the island, she had spotted an advertisement for an early morning horseback ride along the beach, and she had called and signed them up for a trip. It was the only thing she had done. She had left everything for Victor—he had arranged the airline tickets, labeled the suitcases, rented the motorbike, called the desk for extra towels. It was one thing she had done so Victor wouldn't despair of her completely, so she would not despair of herself.

"Let's go for a swim before dinner," said Victor.

And to please him, she said, "Yes, that's a fine idea. It's just what we both need."

The water was so warm she sank into it slowly and swam out with Victor just past where the waves broke. It was slightly too deep for her to stand, so she held on to Victor's back and wrapped her legs around his slick body. People on the beach might have misinterpreted her proximity as sexual, but it didn't matter. This land had more honeymooners than natives and there was a general air of indulgence. Could people mistake them for honeymooners? She and Victor had been married for almost two years, and this was their first real vacation together. They never had a honeymoon. After their wedding they had taken Jeanie to Washington, D.C., where they had stayed with friends and spent their days climbing the infinite, unnecessarily wide stairs to approach all monuments, and waiting on line to get into the Mint and the museums. In previous summers they had gone to Maine, where a colleague of Victor's lent them a lakeside house. The water was cold there and the mosquitoes were large as wasps. Here there were no mosquitoes and the water was sinfully warm. She felt these pleasures were squandered on her—a person who remembered pleasure as a concept but could no longer really feel it—just as a person who has gone deaf can remember but in no way ever hear sound again.

When they came up the beach to the patio, both she and Victor had tar on their feet. They sat by the hotel's foot bath and Victor scrubbed hers clean with a tenderness that reminded her of when she was a little girl and her father would massage her numb toes after she came in from skating. Victor, out of habit, apologized for the tar, as if the oil transports that had polluted the ocean were in part his fault, or that it was his fault that he had brought her here to a place where such things occurred.

In the past, she'd been someone who constantly suffered the imperfections of the world, and Victor, since they first started keeping company after she and Carl were separated, had always tried to smooth the way for her. It was an impossible task; she seemed almost to attract inconvenience. In restaurants she always got the table by the swinging kitchen doors or right underneath the air-conditioning duct. On trains she always got the seat next to the person who smoked in the non-smoker, or the seat where the reading light no longer worked. But now a numbness had taken over everything. Drafts and disturbances were not even noticed. When she brushed against a prickly plant on their way up from the beach, she felt its rough leaves on her skin, but her mind did not connect with the sensation. The message had been lost somewhere in the long route everything took to get to her, a route gouged out by pain.

And the pain was so acute, so formidable, that she consciously held herself as far from it as she could. She worked hard to avoid situations or references that might begin to remind her, might lead her back near the pain. She knew instinctively, like a person with a complex set of fatal allergies, what things to avoid, and she steered her mind instinctively away from danger. She avoided school yards and the girls' section of department stores. At home she drove new routes and sought out new friends. She wasn't always successful, and when she wasn't, a terrible fear would strike her before the pain came, a fear that was almost as bad as the pain itself.

After dinner they strolled, arm-in-arm, just as the honeymooning couples did, along the village's main street. There were a few shops open late, mostly the kind that lured tourists, and Victor was happy when she spotted one that interested her. It was a store that sold shells, shells of all sorts and things made out of shells. There was a crowd of baskets on the floor in the center of the shop, baskets heaped with shells, and the store had a friendly feeling, like a fruit and vegetable store. The rare shells were set on glass shelves along the wall, and even they looked like fruit on display.

Margaret went from basket to basket, lifting out a handful of shells, searching among them for the best example of each type. They all appealed to her. She remembered that when she was young she used to wish she had a tiny head and a long skinny neck so she could peer into them, curl round and round and see the secret that was inside.

"See anything you like?" asked Victor.

"The sand dollars are nice," she said, "but they're $1.98 a piece. That's ridiculous, isn't it? When I was a kid I used to collect them on the beach all the time."

"Well, we're on an island where a cup of coffee costs a dollar," said Victor. "A sand dollar for $1.98 is probably a bargain, and this is an even better bargain, fifteen cents." He held a basket up to her, filled with small shells called bleeding teeth.

"I don't know," she said, and she put her hand on his shoulder, which was a signal that she wanted to leave. "I think I'd rather find some on the beach."

The shopkeeper overheard her. "Not on these beaches," she said. "Almost no shells on these beaches—all the shells in this shop have been imported here."

Outside, Margaret turned to Victor. "It seems wrong somehow, doesn't it, to *buy* a shell?"

"Like buying a bunch of daisies," he said, and for a moment she shared with him a memory of when he had first fallen in love with her and surprised her at work with a bunch of daisies. He had lied to her that he found them growing along the road, even though it was New York City, because he knew she was a woman who did not believe in buying cut flowers, and he was afraid to disappoint her.

This memory sustained them, sustained them long enough so that when they got back to their hotel she was able to make love with him, though still with a joylessness that they both pretended wasn't there. But they made love, for the first time since they had come to the island, for the first time in many weeks, they made love at least.

The next morning she awoke in terror, before the alarm went off. What had she been dreaming of? The Rastafarian on horseback. Galloping past, swooping low, snatching her up. The horse leaped up like Pegasus and flew too high—no oxygen that high, no air.

She got out of bed and pulled open the curtain in front of the sliding glass doors just far enough so she could see out. There was no dawn, only a colorless pre-morning. The ocean in the distance was indistinguishable from the sky.

She got back into bed with Victor, but she could not go back to sleep. Victor, barely awake, sensed her anxiety, held her close. The alarm swept them with sound and was, mercifully, silenced by Victor's quick hand.

"Bad dream?" he asked.

"Yes," she said, "that man on horseback—"

But there was something more, something she had begun to remember when she looked out towards the sea. That wild black horse was like a horse who had run away with her years before. She and Carl were vacationing at Cape Cod, Jeanie was just a baby, and Margaret had gone for a horseback ride along the beach at sunset. Carl had stayed with Jeanie, and Margaret had gone off with the group, waving back at them. As soon as the horses came over the dunes, as soon as they were in sight of the ocean, her horse had broken out of line, had taken off on his own and galloped full out down the length of the beach. He had ignored Margaret, clinging to his back, pulling as hard on the reins as she possibly could, ignored her screams, her terror. He ran the full length of the beach and then trotted back to the stables on his own, Margaret exhausted and shaken on his back.

Carl had been waiting there for her, Jeanie asleep in the baby pack on his back. And Carl had wrapped his big arms around her while she wept with relief, and that night Carl had held her and stroked her and soothed her until she was able to fall asleep.

She did not tell Victor about that. Instead she told him she wasn't feeling very well and would he mind if they didn't go on the riding trip.

"This is a vacation," said Victor, "we don't do anything unless it's something we really want to do." He was awake now.

"But I don't want to disappoint you, I—"

"Me? Sweetheart, I was going along with this to please you. I don't like horseback riding. I don't even like horses."

It was impossible for Margaret to tell what Victor really wanted, really liked. She had thought he had been excited about the riding. But he had probably mustered enthusiasm because she had suggested the trip and he wanted so much to please her. It was possible, she realized, for them continually to do things that neither of them liked but both imagined the other wanted.

In the afternoon they went out on a snorkeling expedition to the coral reef. There were a few honeymooning couples on the boat and one large family. Margaret avoided families as well as she could, as if her tragedy were somehow contagious, and she felt that they would not want her to be near them, as much as to save herself pain. Victor, who understood her game of avoidance and always helped her if he was able to, kept her away from the stern, where the kids congregated, and when they anchored out on the coral reef, he led her off snorkeling far from their splashings and cries. She wanted desperately to thank him for this, for this small part of his vast program of tenderness, and did so, as she often tried to, by seeming to be happy, to be enjoying things.

And this time she found she actually enjoyed herself—by forgetting who she was, what she was, by spying on a totally unfamiliar world, where her troubles did not exist any more than she did. The ocean had always seemed endless to her as she gazed across its surface; now, dangled, tiny above it, she realized that it opened up endlessly in depth, as well. Just beyond the reef was a clean white desert, vast as the sky. The coral reef was as bright and varied as any jungle on earth. Some fish darted in and out around the coral, others swam listlessly above. A jellyfish propelled itself by, like a pale, pulsating heart, and a wave of fish, like tiny flecks of mica, caught the sunlight and swept away with it. Perhaps this was heaven here, and the fish were all the souls. The dead were not angels floating above the clouds—that nonsense, lovely as it had seemed when she was a child—but were immortal parrot fish and skates and tarpon swimming endlessly through this windless world.

Margaret looks out across the ocean. The souls of the dead. She presses against the sand with the palms of both hands. The facts, the simple facts, the litany she has learned by heart, runs through her mind. She had learned it slowly and with effort— learned to say it first in her mind, then learned even more slowly, to believe it. Now she can run it through her mind as effortlessly as she had finally been able, as a child, to run through a C major scale on the piano:

Jeanie was with Carl for the weekend. He took her apple-picking in the country. They went out with a group of people in a pick-up truck. The truck swerved to avoid hitting some-thing on the dirt road—a rock, a turtle. Jeanie, sitting on the lap of a stranger in the back, was thrown out of the truck and landed on the ground. No one else was hurt. Jeanie was dead.

The facts. The procession of them is cool and familiar and bearable. But what she comes back to, what she had been seek-ing in her mind, is the horseback ride. That ride along the beach. She was flying through space even faster than the sound of her own screams. And then, what seemed like days later, the horse, exhausted, had carried her through the dune paths it knew by heart, back to the stable. And there was Carl, waiting for her, and he had gathered her off her horse and held her in his arms. And he was the solid ground under her feet, and she had loved him as fiercely as she loved her own life.

If she had never stopped loving Carl. If she and Carl had not gone their separate ways. If they hadn't arranged for Jeanie to spend two weekends a month with Carl. If Jeanie hadn't been away from her that weekend. If she had stayed with Carl, she would have been with Jeanie all the time, every moment, she would have held her tight—

There is no escape. Margaret hunches close to the sand. She will stop her mind from thinking. She will study the sand, the tiny bits of things, some like hands and feet, some like tiny people. She scoops sand into a mound at her feet. And then she sees something, something large and round and white. A sand dollar? Could it have survived the coral reef, washed up on the beach? She reaches to catch it before the undertow claims it again, but before she can touch it she is knocked backwards off her feet, back onto the sand that is hard as concrete, and the water closes in over her. She fights to find her way up, but she can't tell which way is up. The ocean drags her in deep, and she is spun in the turbulence and then thrown back up on the beach. As she is dragged back through the sand again, her head breaks through to the air, and she is able to choke out the water from her lungs and catch enough air to keep herself alive. The force outside her body is even greater than the force of the pain inside her, as if the ocean had suffered and was expressing some grief even more terrible than her own. But Margaret keeps hold in the sand, and the second wave, milder than the first, retreats without her. Victor comes running down the beach. He lifts her up out of the sand and pushes the wet hair off her face.

"Are you all right?"

"Yes," she manages to say at last, "I'm all right."

Everything hurts her, every surface of skin stings, every joint aches. The resentment, the anger that she was sure was building subtly inside Victor, so secretly it was unknown even to himself, had been expressed with that wave. She has suffered the blows; a score has been equalled. She looks at Victor's face. It is kind and loving, and it will be—she believes this now—that way forever.

What We Save for Last

Ears

We are waiting behind the door, Josef, Alfred K. Hopkins, and me. The door is cracked just enough for us to see the hazard of light, and then it swings open and we walk out into the glare. I could not see beyond the lights if I looked out that way, and I don't look. The noise, which I know is human but which never sounds human to me, builds till it goes beyond sound, till it shakes the floor, the walls, the building itself. I bow my head and walk to my seat, as unobtrusively as I am able, an unobtrusiveness I have been perfecting now for ten years. Dark plain dress, soft plain shoes. Hair neat and straight, pulled back behind my ears—a girl's hairdo, unchanged from when he first saw me, a decade ago.

In eighteen seconds he will begin to play. He always begins precisely on time, even if people are not yet in their seats. He does not do this to reprimand the tardy, as some people have suggested; he is neither arrogant nor eccentric. He does this because if he hesitates one second he may lose all his nerve and flee—and his fear of doing that is as great as his fear of the audience itself. And that is one reason I am here. He turns back, toward the piano. Alfred K. Hopkins is kneading his hands before the keyboard, a habit that both Josef and I dislike and which will no doubt result in Josef firing him, as he has done with so many accompanists before. Josef turns back towards the piano, but it is my face he is looking at, my face that he wants to see once more before he begins. I do not smile. I do not need to smile. He knows the whole range of my thoughts, more complex than any smile could suggest. He sees my face, and then he turns back and lifts his bow so hair meets string.

The difference between a good violinist and a great one is that the good one makes the simple piece seem difficult, the great one makes the difficult piece sound simple. Josef makes the most impossible piece sound effortless. Centuries of composers who set out to create a sonata, a concerto, a capriccio to test a violinist's talents have not been able to produce one measure that doesn't come from Josef's violin as naturally as a melody from the throat of a bird. Even when he was a child, I am told, this was so. He played with an instinct that some dared call divine. He dazzled, he confused, he overwhelmed even those who were listening just for flaws. Some people thought there was some trick, but there was no trick. They analyzed his hand position, his fingering, his bowing, but there was nothing there that they could profit from. There was nothing unusual, no trick, except perhaps the trick of birth, that he, Josef, came into the world with this music already programmed in his fingers, in his mind. And all his life, since he was a small child, people have idolized him for it. Me? I am different. I accept his talent as I accept the talent of squirrels who maneuver through the maples with the perfection of balance, or the clouds that move above them in endless and ever-changing configurations of white against blue.

And it was because of this that he picked me out that first time, years ago. He had come to the conservatory to teach a master class. A dozen students, I among them, had been selected for the privilege of listening to him. I listened to what he said, but I listened more closely to what he played. He picked me out at the end of the class. That girl in the dark dress, he said, that girl with her hair pulled back behind her ears.

And so that night, when he performed on stage, his one concert in our small city, a concert that had been sold out two months in advance, I sat on the stage beside the accompanist and turned the pages. Josef, of course, played from memory—he could memorize a piece if he had heard it just once—but the accompanist, that one, and all of them since, played from sheet music. We had one rehearsal in the auditorium the evening of the concert. The pianist, her face screwed up with a superfluity of emotion, undulated her torso as she played, a habit Josef had already taken a dislike to. She clued me in on my duties with little pokes of her chin.

Before the concert Josef summoned me to his dressing room. He was lying on the couch, his face pale, his hands on his belly. I asked him if he was all right and he assured me that it was nothing, nothing I should think about, he would be fine once he began to play. Alone in the room with him then, I paid attention to his voice. He had been born in America—I knew that—but he had the Russian accent his parents must have spoken with. People, I had heard, thought he cultivated this, but when I got to know him I found out it was something he was totally unconscious of. He simply spoke with the accent he had grown up with and never altered it over time. In truth, he did not really listen to speech and could not hear one accent from another, just as a tone-deaf person cannot hear the difference between a diminished and a perfect fifth.

He had summoned me, he said, because he wanted to explain why he had chosen me. In the class he had seen my face while he was playing. I watched him, he said, not with the look that students usually had, not with a look of devotion, or even admiration. I watched him with a look of possessiveness, a satisfaction, as if I myself had been playing instead of him and was no more amazed by his playing than he was himself.

And when I told him that, yes, it was so, I realized that my life as a musician had changed forever. I had no desire to touch my own instrument ever again. I would be content to listen to him, if I could, and enjoy his music as if I myself had played it.

The stage fright that had attacked him that night dissipated as soon as his first notes sounded. They were not notes worthy of him, they were notes that had been squeezed out with the same kind of effort other musicians require to play. But once his hands recognized their instrument, they slid into their natural song. I watched him. I listened to him. I listened to every note. I had to struggle to keep my mind at all on the piano part so I could reach forward at just the right moment and flip over the page.

Throughout that first concert I listened to Josef, and I suffered for Josef as well. It was as if I was the container for all his fear, and by taking it all inside myself I had freed him to play. It was a fear that was steady and strange and lonely. For the entire time on stage was like time on a far planet, a planet aglow with unnatural lights, and the eyes of the faces in the dark beyond were like flickers of distant celestial bodies in the night sky.

When the second half of the concert was over, I ran to his dressing room. And there, after his fifth curtain call and his encore, he found me weeping.

"And so?" he asked, "something has happened?"

"No nothing," I cried out. "It's nothing. It's just relief."

"You suffered so much?"

"I'm sorry," I said, "I—"

"Hush," he said, "you make it difficult for me to ask you what I need to ask."

And what he asked me was if I would be there to listen to him at each concert that he gave. He needed me, he said, to be his ears. He needed me to listen while he played as he himself could not. While he played he was always anticipating the coming phrase. He heard in his mind only the note that was ahead, not the note he had already played. He depended on my possessiveness. I was the only person who could listen to him as he himself would listen if someone else were playing. He would be the musician, and I, I would be his ears.

"Our world applauds the writer," he said, "not the reader; the artist, not the viewer; the musician, not the audience. But, music, it only exists when it is heard, as words on paper only exist when they are read. As a listener you are as crucial to my playing as I am myself. To make the music, to make it exist, is needed both of us."

I gave up my studies, I gave up my life, the little life I had, and I melded into Josef's, going where he went, cities all over the world, and then hiding out with him in the country between tours. I never played the violin again, and I did not miss it. The pleasure I had always gotten was from listening to music, not from the act of playing it. Josef never discouraged me from playing—quite the opposite—but he accepted my decision and accepts the fact that I am not sorry about it. I had been a good violinist, but I would never have been a great one. There was no reason to regret abandoning such a career.

I was the last of a family of too many daughters, and I had

taken up the violin, I suppose, because I had so much time alone. My siblings were too old to be companions of any sort, my father was too busy to pay attention to any of us, and my mother was tired out from having paid attention to the five who had preceded me.

My father was, and still is, a man of enormous power, although you would probably not know his name. He is obituary editor of an important newspaper, and people with foresight, especially those in advancing years, curry his favor. My father fancies himself a poet and produces poems that have the double fault of being imitative and abstruse. They have been published far more often than they have deserved and treated with excessive tact by critics conscious of their own mortality. My mother always disapproved of my father's poetry, my father disapproved of my mother's fatigue, but they had a rare moment of harmony when they discovered they both disapproved of my choice to attend a conservatory, years ago, and we have seen little of each other in the time since then. It would be unlikely they would ever attend one of Josef's concerts, and even if they did, it is unlikely they would recognize me there on stage, should they notice me at all.

The job of a page turner is a job that is greatly misunderstood. It is not simply a matter of following the music and reaching forward at the exact moment to move a piece of paper quickly, soundlessly, evenly, so that not one note is lost in the procedure. The pages are thin and bodiless, and handling them is like handling leaves in a capricious breeze. A misplaced breath will shatter their order. That is the physical dilemma, the lesser of the two. For a page turner has to cope with the concept that music, sound, is actually connected to that frail page, that there is some correlation between the patterns of ink and the patterns of sound. A page turner has to make herself believe that the sounds that lie in code on one surface of the papers are not the same exact sounds that lie in code on the other side of the page. A page turner has to fight down all rebellious thoughts, thoughts inspired, no doubt, by listening to the musician the pianist is struggling to accompany, a musician who plays without any such intermediary as a printed page.

A page turner has to be obsequious. She has to accept that in the minds of the audience she is less important than the accompanist, than the piano, than even the sheet music itself. When the concert is over the violinist and the pianist bow to the applause, the page turner is done, off-stage, forgotten behind the wings. And that is the ultimate talent. To be so good at what you do that you are not ever noticed. So no one remembers you, no one really even knows that you were there.

Although journalists follow Josef's career with meticulous attention, so far not one has noticed me, noticed the fact that since that first concert, ten years ago, he has never once appeared on stage without me there. Josef, of course, would never let them know my name, and we do our best not to be seen together in public situations where suspicion might be aroused.

Josef guards his privacy with excessive care. He has lived this way, has had to live this way, for as long as he can remember. When he was a child his parents set up an elaborate barricade to enable him to have a bit of private life. His estate in the country, his sanctuary where we retreat after tours as quickly as we can, has never been open to the press; in fact its location has never been divulged. Here Josef, at his happiest, plays in his studio by the french doors, looking out across the garden and the lawns to the woods beyond. The house is modest, but he has allowed himself one luxury, a large indoor pool with a conservatory at one end. Swimming is his only indulgence, he says; it is something close to music. He swims with a smooth and effortless stroke, as fluid as his bowing, and it would not surprise me if the sound of his motion through the water is musical as well. He placates journalists and the public by giving lengthy, thoughtful interviews at the beginning of each new concert season. About his private life he says not one word. He has been married, this is known, but his wife and he have long ago parted ways. She—like the public in general—misinterpreted his shyness as arrogance, his fear as mere eccentricity, and ultimately, she was jealous of his talent. He is a true gentleman and has only courteous things to say about her. Although he feels sad she understood him so little, he does not hold this against her and has confessed to me that perhaps he did not understand her very well either. His weapon against the press—should they try to invade his privacy—is that he may turn into a recluse completely. They accept what he extends, perhaps knowing how hard it is for him to submit to those interviews, afraid that he might withdraw them all.

Josef's relationships with his accompanists have always provoked journalistic interest. Although he has always been generous in his comments about pianists he's worked with, they have not always been so about him. He has a reputation of being a difficult person to please, but it is the pianists who gradually turn sulky. Josef and I both see the piano as an inferior instrument to a violin, a piece of furniture as opposed to a living thing you cradle against your body, hold against your skin. But he is careful not to let the pianist see this prejudice. When he plays with a pianist he shares the stage equally with him or her, but all his accompanists, even those who start off with the greatest gratitude to be allowed to play with him at all, end up feeling upstaged. But how could they not? His great talent eclipses any they might demonstrate.

With all his accompanists, in the decade we've been together, a kind of staleness sets in after a season together. Then, gradually, things grow thorny between them. The accompanist demands more and more—money, print size, whatever it is—and he grows more and more aware of eccentricities of theirs which have become exaggerated over time. Perhaps, (I've thought this, though I have never confessed this, not even to him) he grows uncomfortable with them when he begins to be afraid they have begun to guess something about us.

Us. He holds us as secret as he holds anything in his life. How could he explain to anyone what we are to each other? To whom could he say, "she is essential to me; she is my ears?" And what would people think? When an older man links himself with a younger woman, they have some tawdry scenario all worked out. They would think our connection was based on something entirely different from what it was. Would they understand that our closest moments together, our moments of greatest passion, are those moments when we face together that dark sky, when he turns and I hold my face for him to see, and I soothe his terror and give him the courage to lift his bow and place it on the strings?

In our years together, he and I have grown closer in all things, more alike. We have come to have similar taste in color, in food. We both are extremely sensitive to fluctuations in temperature and travel always with a range of clothing to accommodate all weather. We are both highly susceptible to cold, and I test the temperature on stage for him before each concert. Often he will wear long underwear under his tails, thin wool underwear that no one could ever detect. Even though he ends up sweating at the end of each concert, he is cold at the beginning, a condition which worsens as he gets older. And we are both getting older. Josef's hair is thinning in the back, though the sides are swept out to give an appearance of fullness. I am no longer a girl at the conservatory, though I still wear my hair that way, and from a distance, I must still look like one.

Some critics have suggested that those first inferior notes Josef plays are signs of age, but that is not the case; it has always been that way. He is getting older now, that is a fact, but this affects only his energy to concertize, not the quality of his playing. When he plays, he is inexhaustible, vigorous, possessed. If you compare his performances now with recordings from his youth you would hear no decline. We talk more and more, though, about him retiring. He certainly has no need of more money or fame, and the traveling and performing are wearing him out. But when we begin to consider giving up the next tour, he shakes his head. "What about you?" he asks. "What about you?" For he worries that my job is as important as his, that his retirement is tied to mine. I tell him that my job is not that important to me, but he worries that the performances are essential and that he can't give up. He knows that I would never leave him while he needed me. The few times I have been sick and unable even to sit onstage he has canceled his performance, claiming the sickness as his own. He cannot play, he insists, without me there. Would I stay with him if he retired, if he did not need me so?

The public believes Josef will go on performing forever because it is his way of showing gratitude for his great gift. If they knew how he suffered before each performance, they would say it was his way of working off his guilt for having been given such talent. But they don't know that he accepts his talent, just as I accept his talent. He is playing not for them but for me. He plays to keep me employed; I am employed to keep him playing. It goes in a circle. We can do nothing for ourself alone, and nothing for each other without it being for ourself as well. I wonder if this is what love creates, or if this is what creates love.

He is now playing the last measures of the Brahms, the last piece. He always saves Brahms, my favorite, for the end. He will come out on stage again when the audience cries out for an encore and do a showy Paganini or Wieniawski, but he ends his real concert on Brahms because it is what I like, and after the Brahms, my job for the evening is done.

The piece is over. I walk off-stage quickly. Josef and Alfred K. Hopkins step forward to meet the audience's cries. Then they retreat, for a breather, out the side stage door. There are people backstage waiting to greet Josef, and I am pushed together with them. He smiles and tries to catch his breath before he has to go back on stage once more. He looks around for me and finally spots me in the crowd and nods. "Thank you," he says to me, courteously, just as if I were an ordinary page turner, a student hired for the evening, someone he has never seen before, may never see again. And the people who are there, who hear him say this, never know the truth, never know who I really am and what he is really saying when he sees my face.

Forbidden Waters

Her name was Eleanore, but a name like Jean or Jo would have suited her better. She was a lean woman, with short blond hair and narrow blue eyes that would have been at home in a man's face. Eleanore seems like a name for a matronly woman, a woman like my mother was then, plump and soft-eyed. I saw Eleanore only that one time, yet her features are as clear to me now, years later, as the features of people I know well. I can even picture her hands on the oars, her long, tan fingers, fingernails filed straight across.

But I'm getting ahead of myself. This is a story about reservoirs, those special bodies of water that are set aside for drinking water and protected by law. There was a reservoir near the house where I grew up, and there is a reservoir near the house my husband and I have just bought. This reservoir is forbidden to swimmers, boaters, and fishermen, forbidden to everything except, perhaps, looking. No Trespassing signs are posted all around, but the signs are old and there is a path along the shore made by trespassers before us. The reservoir of my childhood was forbidden to swimmers and picnickers, but licensed fishermen were allowed to cast their lines from the shore, and some were even given permits to keep rowboats there.

I never liked fishing for itself, but I enjoyed going fishing with my father. Sometimes we cast from a favorite spot on shore; sometimes we borrowed the rowboat of someone he knew from work. Fishing is one of the few things in the world where you can sit and do nothing and nobody bothers you. You don't even have to talk.

The water level in the reservoir was controlled by a dam at the far end. The water was pumped to the city, an hour away. The houses near the reservoir got drinking water from their own wells. Ours had a high iron content, and everything white that we owned looked as if it had been rinsed in tea. People who lived in our town and commuted to the city to work got to drink the reservoir water during the day, but no one in my family did. My father taught social studies at the high school in a neighboring town, and my mother didn't work at all. This was the late fifties and it wasn't peculiar then for a college-educated woman like my mother not to work. She had stayed home to raise her family, and even though I, the youngest, was in school all day, she still stayed home. It was almost as if she hadn't realized her children had grown up, and everyone was too tactful to point it out to her.

The water in the reservoir fluctuated according to rainfall and according to the needs of the city. One year the water was so high it drowned all the young trees on the periphery. During one drought the reservoir was emptied. All that was left was the original stream that fed it, finding its way through the huge depression. Someone built a stepping-stone path across the belly, and grass grew, like a field. But that was an unusual year. For most of the time, and for the year that matters to this story, the water came up to the top of the concrete footings for the bridge.

I am certain that my mother never knew where we actually went when my father and I set off together, wearing our most disreputable clothes. If she had seen our favorite fishing spot, she probably would not have let even my father go, for we had to climb over the bridge railing, edge along the concrete footings, then scramble over some boulders to get there. This was the spot, my father said, where the water was deepest. Here were the pools where the bass lurked, those elusive fish whose name even now gives me the chills, for I remember how my father used to say it, his voice rising and falling as he spun out the vowel, his eyes widening with the sound. He almost never caught any, however. In fact he rarely caught any fish from shore, and what he caught — mostly sunnies — he usually threw back. From the rowboat he occasionally caught a perch. Once he brought one home for my mother to cook, but after an elaborate cleaning procedure there were still scales, like mica, which caught in our teeth, and endless bones. The only fish my mother liked to cook was filet of sole, which isn't really a fish at all.

What We Save for Last

My father taught me everything he knew about fishing. He taught me how to hunt for night crawlers, how to bait a hook, how to cast, and how to be patient. I was good at everything except baiting the hook, even though my father promised me it didn't hurt the worm. I always turned away when my father caught a fish and went to work to get the hook out of its mouth, my hand shielding my own lips.

My father also taught me how to row. When I was little, he would sit beside me and have me work one oar; when I was older, he had me row myself. He taught me how to row with oars together in what he called "Indian style," and he taught me how to maneuver around rocks and untangle fishing line from dead branches. Sometimes I would row and he would trawl. Sometimes he rowed and I would lean far back off the boat and trail my fingers in the water. I was filled with longing to swim in that water, and on hot days it seemed like a particular privation to see all that cool water around us and not be able to lower my body into it. I was a good swimmer—years of lessons at the Y pool—and I had fantasies about cutting across the reservoir, my father in the rowboat keeping pace with me, the way I imagined Channel swimmers were followed by their escorts.

The boat we borrowed was painted green on the outside and blue on the inside. It was chained to a tree in a pine grove beside the reservoir, the chain looped through the oarlocks and the handles of the life-preserver cushions we sat upon. The boat was just small enough for us to be able to turn it over, drag it to the water, and get it afloat. It was always heavier when it was time to bring it in, and the pine needles stuck to the wet hull. There were a few other fishermen around, and some of the boats were nearly camouflaged under more than a season of pine needles and leaves.

One late Friday afternoon in September, when it was still warm enough to fool yourself into thinking summer wasn't really over and school hadn't begun, my father and I headed down to the reservoir to fish for a while before dinner. Looking back on it now, certain aspects of the scene stand out for me, though I don't think I really noticed them at the time. It's as if the whole afternoon was preserved fairly objectively in my memory, and only now, in retrospect, do I observe things that I passed over then.

The reservoir was actually walking distance from our house, but we always drove, because the trunk and backseat of my father's car were full of gear. My mother ran a tidy house—even the basement and the garage—and my father's old car, which she never drove or rode in, was the one place where he could keep things as he liked. We didn't take much with us to our fishing spot or when we went out in the boat, but my father liked having the car nearby so he'd have access to extra rods and reels and tackle and rags and pails.

That afternoon when we got our regular parking spot along the road, my father saw another car already there and hesitated pulling off. It was a brief hesitation, and I make note of it only now, as I think about what might have been going on in my father's head. At the time I was impatient to go fishing and annoyed that anyone else was there. I liked to think of the reservoir as our place. I liked to imagine we owned it all: that long, narrow body of water, the surrounding pine forest, even the hills beyond.

There was a woman standing by the opened trunk of the car. She seemed surprised to see us. Then she waved and my father waved. We pulled off the road behind her car and got out, and my father brought me over to introduce us. Eleanore, my father explained, taught math at his school, and she was the owner of the boat we had been using all these years. It had never occurred to me that the owner of the boat was a woman. In fact it never occurred to me that women did—or even could—own boats.

My father and I had been planning to take the boat out ourselves that afternoon, but it was clear Eleanore had the same idea. My father told her we'd be just as happy fishing from shore.

"Why don't we all go out in the boat together?" she asked.

My father looked over at me and then back to Eleanore.

What We Save for Last

"Come on," she said. "There's room enough for the three of us." She moved her rod out of the way and slammed the hood of her trunk.

We got our gear together and walked single file on the path through the woods, Eleanore in front of me, my father behind. Eleanore wore navy blue sneakers and jeans and a faded blue workshirt with the cuffs folded up. From the back, she could have been a boy. This was a time when my mother and most of the women I knew always wore skirts. Of course they never went fishing.

We walked silently through the pine forest to the boat. My father and I stood aside while Eleanore undid the lock and untangled the chain from the oars and the cushions. Then she and my father lifted the boat and carried it to the water. My father held the boat steady while I climbed in and took my place in the small third seat in the bow. As we headed out from shore, I caught Eleanore looking at me, smiling, as if waiting for me to say something. So I said, "This is a nice boat. I like its colors."

"Thank you," she said. "I painted it green on the outside to reflect the water and blue on the inside to reflect the sky."

I didn't say anything after that. My father rowed out towards the center of the reservoir, and I listened to the oars moving in the oarlocks, like the sound of a familiar bird, and I listened to the oars moving the water, the boat moving through the water. What was peculiar about the outing was how quiet we all were. My father bragged to Eleanore about my rowing and my casting and urged me to take a turn at the oars, or in the stern, trawling. But I shook my head. They seemed content to let the subject drop, and we all fell into our silences.

It was hot out in the middle of the reservoir. More than ever, I wished I could dive off the boat and swim. I scooped up water and splashed my face and the back of my neck. My father took off his shirt. The hair on his arms was flattened with sweat, and droplets of sweat, perfectly formed like droplets of oil, glistened on his shoulders. Eleanore had taken off her work shirt, and underneath she was wearing a red-and-white striped polo. She had small, widely set breasts, and I could tell she wasn't wearing a bra. She slicked her hair back with water and held her face up to the sun.

My father rowed to the south end of the reservoir, then he and Eleanore exchanged places and she rowed back north. Neither of them caught any fish. Eleanore got a few bites, but the fish took her worm and got away. My father thought he had a big one, but when he reeled it in, he had just a rotting branch. We headed back to shore while the evening gathered around us and the reservoir began swallowing the sun.

I carried the tackle boxes and the rods and reels, and my father and Eleanore flipped the boat over and carried it back to its place. My father ran the chain through the oarlocks and cushion handles, and Eleanore locked everything up. As we left, my father slapped the boat on its side, the way you'd slap a horse at the end of a long ride.

We walked back to our cars with me in the lead this time. My father was usually slow about stowing his gear in the car, but this time he stuffed it in without ceremony. Eleanore was ready to leave even before us. She didn't really say good-bye, she just gave her horn three little taps as she took off.

At dinner my father said nothing about Eleanore and I didn't either. My mother asked us how our fishing went, and he said fine, the way he always did, and my mother didn't ask anything more about it.

There are two things, in retrospect, that stand out about that afternoon. One is the way Eleanore and my father handled the boat together, the way they lifted it and carried it and laid it in the water. They worked with a smoothness that could have come only from experience and practice, or perhaps from some remarkable instinct. The other thing is the kind of quiet they shared that day. They were quiet the way my father and I were quiet when we were fishing alone.

————

Today my husband and I walked around the reservoir near our house. Like the reservoir of my childhood, the water is in safekeeping for a city far away. There is a diminutive brick building with a green metal roof at one end of the reservoir. At one time it may have been used as a water works office, but it has been deserted for years. Perhaps the water in the reservoir is no longer actually pumped off to the city. Perhaps the reservoir has been forgotten by everyone except for the hikers who come through the woods.

It was the hottest day of the summer, the hottest day since we moved to our new house. My husband wanted to throw off his clothes and go swimming. I looked out at the water. It was so clear I could see the intricacies of each rock, and when some sunnies darted close to the shore I could see the movement of their gills, the beating of their hearts. I wanted to plunge into the water, plunge in and swim across, just as I had wanted to swim across that other reservoir, years ago. But the message on the No Trespassing signs, barely legible with age, stayed with me. I pleaded with my husband to continue our walk.

"You can do as you like," he said, "but I'm going in."

He took off his clothes and side-stepped down the slope into the water. When the water level reached his waist, he pushed forward and let the water take the weight of his body. He dipped his head in once and came up slowly. The water was so clear I could see the hairs lifted up on his arms and legs. His rear end and the soles of his feet were luminously white. He swam out a distance, then he turned towards me again.

"Come in," he said. "It's perfect."

I could smell the coolness of the water. I could imagine it soothing each cell of my hot skin. But I stood there, watching, unable to follow.

When I married my husband, I promised that I would tell him everything, always. It was my second marriage, and I wanted a fullness, an honesty, what I thought of as a purity, I hadn't had the first time around. I wanted to be able to tell him everything I thought and everything I felt. Withholding, I had learned in my first marriage, was not very much better than lying.

But I haven't told him about Eleanore, and I think now that to withhold this small tale is less a sin against love than it would be a sin to tell my father's secret. I tell myself it will not hurt us, my husband and me, if I don't share with him this memory.

———————

What was between them?

I don't know for sure if my father was ever unfaithful to my mother. My guess is that he wasn't. My father's life and Eleanore's life overlapped there, in that blue and green rowboat, the way people's lives so often overlap. And that afternoon I just happened to be there with them in that small boat, there with them and their desire.

Memorial Day

My daughter is wearing French braids for the occasion. They have a configuration I find baffling, but for her sake I have tried to master the technique. Her hair is fine as an infant's, and a multitude of hidden bobby pins are required to hold things together. I am not sure if the impetus for such a hairdo comes from a friend at school or from a desire to please Caleb who has come up to see her perform today. What she has forgotten is that her hair is covered by a hat, so he hasn't yet had a chance to notice. He was late, of course, and missed seeing her before she joined the ranks of junior high school brass players in their uniforms: black pants, red blazers, and red berets with pompoms perched on the top.

Caleb still hasn't noticed my hair. When he first saw me he gave me a quick second look, scowled a bit, then as if reassuring himself I was the same person, said nothing at all. I've had straight hair all my life and finally got a permanent. When Sally first saw it, she burst into tears, but she has gotten used to it since. I haven't. I feel ridiculous. My face was never meant for curls, nor my heart.

Caleb didn't catch up with us until the second cemetery. He came running up, trenchcoat flapping, with that bewildered, self-incriminating look he adopts to thwart criticism. This town has four cemeteries: one Protestant, one Catholic, one secular, and one small graveyard which doesn't profess to anything except antiquity. The plan is for the band to march from cemetery to cemetery and at each one play the "Star Spangled Banner" and stand through a tribute to the War Dead pronounced by a septuagenarian member of the American Legion. The kids like it because at the end of the speech two rifles are fired off. I'm sure they're filled with blanks, but the kids have circulated a rumor that real bullets are used and that one year the two old soldiers picked each other off.

Caleb stands next to me in the crowd of parents and townspeople, his head bent, a solemn look on his face. As soon as the rifles have been fired and the band has started to move on, he turns to me:

"The traffic was impossible," he says. "It took me an hour just to get to the highway, another three to get here."

In my mind I hear my familiar response: "You know it's always like that; you should have left earlier." But I don't say anything out loud. I don't want to make this visit an unpleasant one for Sally's sake. Or mine.

"Was Sally upset that I missed seeing her before they started?" Caleb asks.

"I'm sure she'll be happy you were able to make it at all," I say.

It starts drizzling as we walk to the next cemetery. It's been drizzling on and off all day, but Sally told me that they go on playing, no matter what. A sort of soldier's philosophy. Some of the parents have had the foresight to bring umbrellas. I turn up the collar of my coat.

"Are those new glasses?" Caleb asks me.

I shake my head and smile. Sally will set him right when he takes her out for dinner this evening. When he next speaks to me alone he'll apologize for not having noticed my hair and attempt a compliment. Since we have separated he's been conscientious about such things.

This third cemetery, which dates from the early eighteenth century, is the only one I've ever been in before. The tombstones are weathered marble and sandstone in slightly uneven rows facing away from town. Though they mark the graves of babies who never lived long enough to learn to walk, as well as the soldiers of history book wars, they do not really inspire thoughts of death. The setting is too picturesque, the dates too remote. The cemetery is surrounded by a wrought-iron fence, and the onlookers have to wait outside. There is barely enough room inside the enclosure for the whole band to fit without treading on someone's grave. As they file out Sally catches Caleb's eye.

"Daddy!" she whispers, and waves her trumpet. My attendance is taken for granted. She began working on Caleb weeks in advance to get him to come up for this occasion. He said he was reluctant to drive anywhere on Memorial Day weekend, but she won him over. She had brought her trumpet to the city on some of the weekends she had gone down to be with him, but he has never seen her play it in performance before. Band is her favorite activity at school. She loves all the rituals, the distribution and collection of sheet music, practicing marching in the gym, and especially wearing the uniforms, the polyester blazer with the gold epaulets.

Caleb walks beside me to the next cemetery.

"I wasn't able to book a room anywhere nearby," he says. "How do you feel about putting me up for the night?"

I look at him quickly, to catch the expression on his face. "It doesn't have to be anything like that," he says.

I wait a while before I answer. "I think it might confuse Sally."

"Well, give it a second thought, would you?"

"All right," I say.

This last cemetery has an arched gateway with its name, Maple Grove, cut into the stone. As soon as the band gets into formation, the drizzle turns to rain. I look out across acres of graves—confections of marble, ornamental shrubs. We seem such a small group of people, so greatly outnumbered by the dead. Suddenly the rain is an incontrovertible downpour. The parents fly to the cover of trees while the kids play stoically on, until the the band leader reaches the the limit of his own stoicism and directs them all to the covered porch of the pink granite mausoleum. They can barely fit there with all their instruments, and there is a bit of pushing between the boys and girls. They are a remarkable sight: their bright red jackets against the pink stone.

When I was Sally's age I played in my school band. Standing in the midst of my friends, waiting for the cue to lift my clarinet to my lips, I felt protected by our numbers and by the brilliance and volume of the music. My life seemed long and filled with potentially certain happy events. I never thought it possible that beneath the surface of the adult lives I was familiar with there could be such sadness and pain. I thought that only war brought casualties, not loss of love.

"I guess it's too far for me to run back to my car for an umbrella," says Caleb. He takes off his trenchcoat and holds it up behind me. "Here, take a side," he says.

I take the edge of the trenchcoat and we make a canopy over our heads. It is the closest I have been to Caleb in months. The inside of his coat smells warm and familiar, like a house I once lived in. Sally, standing with her classmates on the steps of the mausoleum, pretends she doesn't notice. But I know she has noticed. It is almost as if she has wished this, orchestrated this. It is almost as if her desperate hope has pushed our bodies close together.

Luba by Night

She's found my house all right. After I hear the doorbell ring, I stand by the stairway, hand on the bannister. I've been waiting for her in my study. It would have been too childish to watch for her from an upstairs window. Her voice on the phone had been a whispery little girl's voice, with a hint of a British accent, not that he'd been British, but he'd had an accent like that. I'd pictured her willowy and fair-haired, to match her voice, and while I wait in the hall before I open the door, I imagine her on the other side of it. I wait until she rings again. I keep her waiting like this, control this small space of her time. Neither of us really knows what the other looks like. I have seen a photograph of her when she was a small child, sitting in a garden chair with her feet straight in front, out of focus. Perhaps she's seen a photograph of me, but if it was one of his, if he'd kept any, it's twenty years old, at least. I used to wear my hair long in those days, with bangs across the front.

When I open the door she steps right in and embraces me. It is not a personal embrace, but obviously the way she usually greets people, and then she stands back a bit.

"I'm Luba," she says, and smiles.

She is not anything like the person I had imagined. Fidelity to my image makes her seem, at first, like an imposter. Although she's fair-haired, she's heavyset. I'm afraid to look too hard at her, to search for the features that she inherited from him. When she wriggles out of her jacket I realize that she has breasts, large breasts, which surprises me. It was something I had never thought about one way or another when I worked to conjure her. It was as if I had forgotten that she was actually a woman, this girl Luba, this daughter of his.

———

What should I do about the ring? This morning I found it in the back of a drawer. I knew it was there, but I'd had no reason to open that drawer for years. The drawer was so deep, and the ringbox so far in back, that to reach it you had to open the drawer farther than it was ever intended and risk it falling out. But I knew I had put the box there, and my hand searched back and drew it out into the light. I could not resist taking the ring out of the box and holding it up by the window so the sapphire filled with the morning. If I were a different sort of woman I would have thrown the ring into the river. But I was neither courageous enough nor foolish enough to do that. All I had the courage to do at the time was take the ring off my finger and put it away and let the sapphire die a slow death in the far back corner of my drawer.

———————

When Luba first called she told me she had a job with the summer theatre in town. She wasn't an actress, she was quick to point that out, she was a set and lighting designer. Well, she added, somewhat breathlessly, that's what she sort of hoped to be. Actually she was just a general assistant, one of the many college kids the theatre took on to paint scenery, sell tickets, work the lights. She'd been in town for three weeks before she phoned me, so it was possible we could have passed on the street or brushed up against each other in a store. I know she wasn't spying on me. It simply hadn't occurred to her to call me before then. But I was thinking of this when I kept her waiting at my door. Let her wait, I thought.

———————

I sit across from Luba at the dinner table. It's easier to look at someone while they're busy doing something, like eating. The places at the head and foot of the table are conspicuously empty.

To earn extra money, Luba tells me, she works four nights a week as a salad chef at a local restaurant.

"Mostly all I do is cut things up," she says. "The salad is just

What We Save for Last

greens with a few slices of tomato and some croutons on the top—they try to make it look better by using different kinds of lettuce and cabbage. I like slicing up the cabbage best. It's purple and white and looks like a cross-section of the brain, you know?"

I nod.

"The salads I make go in the refrigerator and then they're taken out just before lunch the next day. It's sort of cheating because the diners think the salads are fresh, and they aren't really."

Luba's long hair is honey-colored, soft and fine as a child's. A good haircut would help it look thicker and fuller, but it's clear Luba hasn't been to a professional stylist in years, if ever. She lets her hair fall about her shoulders, fall across her face. Obviously she thinks it is more beautiful than it is, or else she thinks of herself as someone who needs long hair to hide behind, whose long hair is her only seductive tool. She's quite oblivious to the potential of her breasts; in fact she hunches over, as if she's embarrassed that they are there.

"Did you drive out here?"

"I don't have a car," she says. "I took the bus. Usually I get around by bike—I bought a used one first thing when I arrived—but it's in the shop being repaired. It was only twenty dollars, so I have to put a little money into it, I guess. You see it had this problem that it didn't quite steer the way you wanted it to. It kept wanting to pull a little to the right. Like a horse."

"Do you ride?" I ask.

"Where I grew up," she said, "Everyone rides. It's just one of those things. Except Dad, of course. He hates horses, says he was bitten by one once and they have the meanest teeth of any animal he's ever met. But you know that, don't you? Didn't that happen to him when he was out riding with you?"

I search my mind quickly but can't remember anything of the sort. I'd been interested in horses when I was young, myself, but hadn't had anything to do with them for years. And as far as I could remember, her father and I never went riding together. What could she be thinking of? Or he? Is it possible that the one anecdote that she has connected with my name, the one little story that has been salvaged from the past, has nothing to do with me at all?

"Must have been someone else," I say, but Luba just shrugs. It's not very important to her, one way or the other.

She is round-faced, this Luba, and doesn't look at all like her father at first glance. But she has his eyes, pale greenish-gray eyes with one lid sagging a little in the corner, something that was more pronounced when he was tired. She must be tired now. And her teeth are his, too. Straight, white, aristocratic teeth. I watch her eat.

———————

"That was a perfectly marvelous dinner," says Luba. It's an expression she's obviously fond of, for she's already used it to describe first my house, then my garden. Since it was just the two of us, I'd made scampi, which is one of the few special things I know how to cook.

Now we are in the kitchen and she's helping me clean up while the coffee gets made. She has a huge amount of energy—both verbal and physical, and she's thrown herself into the task with vigor. I have the feeling that if I just stayed in there talking she would go on to clean all the counters, scour out the sink, and wash the floor without quite realizing what she was about.

"My Dad told me once he read that some Indian tribes wouldn't eat turkey because they thought it was a stupid and cowardly creature and were afraid, by eating it, they'd acquire its faults. I wonder what they would have thought of shrimp."

Fortunately it's a rhetorical question, and she goes right on scrubbing the pot I'd left to soak. I'm thinking about her father telling her this, imagining how he would relate the anecdote. When we talked about him at dinner—for how could we have avoided talking about him?—she'd told me mostly general things, facts about his work and his life. This is the first thing

What We Save for Last

she's said about him that's given him any life, that's made me
feel his presence in my house.

The question is, how much does Luba know? It's almost impossible to find out without actually asking her, and of course I
can't do that. The difficulty is that she is totally nonjudgmental.
She lives, it seems, a rather free life, and she's naively accepting
and unsuspicious, like a Flower Child from the generation past.
When people are nonjudgmental it's harder to read them. They
don't struggle to avoid topics that make them uncomfortable,
nor do they tempt fate, nibbling at the edges of forbidden
subjects. Luba talks about her father as if he were just an old
friend of mine, nothing more, which is either because that's all
she knows, or because in her mind, friendship and love are not
separate things, the one comfortable and undemanding, the
other fraught with anguish.

Anguish. It's clear that Luba's had no taste of it. She speaks of
a boyfriend of hers, but she speaks of him with casual pleasure,
without longing. As for her future, she has no real plans, but
uncertainty isn't troubling to her. She's fickle. She's full of half-
baked ideas. She may go back to college in the fall, she tells me.
Or she may go to Europe. She's been to France and England
with her father, but she's always wanted to go to Italy. Don't I
think everyone should see Venice while they're still young?

What did he think I'd do with her then, this daughter of his?
He didn't actually send her to me; what he did was ask her to
look me up when she was out here. What did he expect me to
do? Didn't he imagine it was possible that I would reach across
the table, as we sat there eating, take her neck in my hands and
squeeze it hard, not to squeeze the life out, but just to give myself the satisfaction of knowing that I could if I wanted to?

We settle in the livingroom with our coffee and dessert. Luba takes her coffee with lots of sugar, lots of milk. The dessert is a slice of cantaloupe cradling a scoop of ice-cream.

Once when her father and I were shopping at the supermarket together, he saw me shaking a melon and asked what I was up to. I told him if you heard the seeds rattling, that meant the melon was ripe. He laughed and told me there were two proper ways to test a melon. The first was to smell it; the second was to press your thumbs against the place where the stem broke off, feel the softness of the navel. I picture him holding a honeydew melon, his nose against its flesh.

"Delicious melon," says Luba. I notice that she has finished hers, has in fact eaten much closer to the skin than I ever do.

"There's more in the kitchen," I say. "Would you like another piece?"

"Oh, no thanks," says Luba. "That was just perfect."

"You know," I say, "if you're planning to take the bus back, we should take a look at the schedule. On Sundays they tend to stop running early."

I go into the study and find a schedule in one of the cubbyholes of my desk. I'm right, the buses don't run late on Sundays. In fact, Luba's already missed the last one. I'll have to give her a ride back, I think, but then I remember that my husband has the car, and he won't be back till tomorrow night.

When I go back to the livingroom with the schedule in my hand, Luba's looking at a photograph of my husband and me dancing at our wedding reception. It's in a frame that is a mirror so the viewer's face frames the picture as well. We are not the sort of people who put photographs of ourselves around our house, but this was a gift from my husband's brother, a tongue-in-cheek sort of gift, a photograph of my husband, a non-dancer, caught dancing. It is the sort of picture, proof of marital happiness, that I would have felt absurd setting out on purpose for Luba's visit, but I am glad that it happens to be there. Luba doesn't ask about the photograph, just places it back on the shelf.

What We Save for Last

"We have a guest room," I say. "How would you feel about staying overnight?"

———

My husband is out of town for three days, helping his mother move into a nursing home. I hadn't set it up to have Luba over when he wasn't here, it just worked out that way. Part of me wanted him to be here, so I could show him off to her—my husband is a handsome and charming man—so she would tell her father that. But knowing the power of mysteries, part of me wanted him to remain mysterious. And I was afraid of meeting Luba in his presence, afraid of how I would feel when I met her. She wouldn't guess it, for I have a way of being cordial when I am nervous, which strangers don't recognize, but my husband would. He would wonder what it was about this girl that made me feel that way.

I've told my husband about Luba, of course. But he sees the incidents of life as just a series of things that shape the future, no one of them exerting any more power than any other.

———

I offer Luba one of my nightgowns to wear to bed, but she says she always sleeps in the nude. Does she feel particularly at home with me to say this, or is this just her way? When I was her age I would have accepted the proffered nightgown and not worn it if I had chosen not to. Though even if I were the sort of person who slept naked in my own bed, in someone else's bed I would have wanted something between me and the unfamiliar sheets.

Did I want his daughter to wear my nightgown to have my scent against her skin, to have her scent embedded in the cloth? Does her body smell like his?

———

Luba helps me carry the cups and dishes back into the kitchen. We have been talking more about traveling.

"I think sometimes I'd like to go to Russia," Luba says. "My grandmother was Russian. I have her name."

"I know," I say. "I've met your grandmother."

"You did?"

And that's the first clue I have that perhaps he has not told her all.

"She was a bizarre sort of lady, wasn't she?" asks Luba.

I laugh. "What I found strange was the way she kept referring to this person Philip, as if he were a living member of the family. And only afterwards did your father tell me that it was his identical twin, who'd died in infancy."

"You know about that?" asks Luba. "I thought that was some weird family story my father never told anyone."

And then I'm sure.

———

The notion of twins raises all sort of possibilities. There would be two men, then, that I could have fallen in love with. And if one transgressed, there would still be one left for me. Or would they both have transgressed, leaving two Lubas in their wake?

Twice as much love. Twice as much pain.

And if I were twins I could have had two lives. The life with him, the life I had instead.

———

The guest room is a small room next to my study. If my husband and I had had a child, this would have been the child's room. It was used for children by the people who owned the house before us, and we've left the same wallpaper on the walls: white with blue flowers, and around the top, a blue border with white sheep. The quilt is a log cabin pattern in blues, lavenders, pinks. I won it in a raffle to raise money for the local historical society. It is the only thing I've ever won in my life. Sometimes, when I've worked late the night before, I go into the guest room to take a nap, and it feels like I'm in a room in someone else's house.

After Luba has gone to bed, I go to my study to read. It is very late when I decide to go to bed. It is a warm evening, and Luba has left the door open a crack. I stand in the doorway and let my eyes get accustomed to the darkness. I hear her breathing as she sleeps, and after a while I can see well enough to watch her body under the sheet, watch it rise and fall with her breath.

I think of myself lying next to her father, listening to his heart beating, the patterns of his breath. I had thought, then, that I would have him next to me all the nights of my life, that his breathing would be as familiar to me as my own.

She is sleeping still. "Luba," I say, softly, "your father told me about it himself. Not because he was afraid I'd find out from someone else, but because he thought it would seem less important that way. A last fling, he called it, laughing, hoping he could get me to laugh, too, for wasn't it a feeble thing to do, a classic weak, male thing to do?

"Except that she got pregnant—by design, my friends who knew her told me—the oldest trick in the book.

" 'Well, you'll have to marry her, then,' I said.

" 'What do you want me to do?' he asked. 'Ruin my life?'

" 'No,' I said, 'I just want to keep you from ruining mine.'

"They stayed married long enough for me to think they might stay married forever. By the time they were apart, by the time you started splitting your life between their two houses, my life had gone off on its own. Don't let anyone tell you there's no such thing as too late."

I steal close to the bed and look down on Luba. She is sound asleep. I think: her body is those years. That time, that whole part of my life, has made this: her shoulders, her hair, her cheekbones, her hands.

I watch Luba's body move with her breathing. I feel my own move with my own breath.

Reparations

There had been three of them then, and there are three of them now. She recognizes the car, an olive-green sedan, sunk low to the ground. When she called the police she had been embarrassed to discover she didn't know the make or the year. All she had been sure of was that it was an American car with four doors. When she was a child she had known all the cars—makes, models, years—and she would call them out on the highway when she went on trips with her parents. Her father bragged about this to his friends. It was funny to think that of all the things she had done in her life this was the one accomplishment her father seemed proudest of. It is funny to be thinking about her father, now. Paralyzed by his latest stroke, he is slumped over in a wheelchair in an old-age home, unable to help her, as helpless as she feels herself.

The car drives slowly past the house, then backs up to her driveway and turns in. Her first thought is to make a run for the house, but she knows she is too far from the front door, and she does not want to be seen running, does not want to turn her back to them. And she probably couldn't run, even if she decided to. She is too frightened even to move to brush the soil off her knees.

The car goes up to the end of the driveway, then it backs around to face out again. The headlights are elongated ovals, like the heavy-lidded eyes of a seductive woman. Everything is rusty except for the chrome hood ornament, which glints in the sunlight. From her distance it looks like a beast with its forepaws raised in a boxing pose, a sort of pugilist leopard. She is glad she didn't run for the house. She feels somewhat safer outdoors, under the broad expanse of sunlight, in full view of the road.

The car poses for a few minutes with its engine running. Then the engine is shut off and three doors open at once and three young men step out. Her instinct is to crouch, to hope she will not be seen, but the only thing between her and them is a stretch of lawn and the garden, with a half dozen flats of marigolds and petunias. She grips the trowel in her hand.

It seems significant that they should come now and find her here in the garden, working to repair the damage they'd done. They had come at dusk. She had been on the front porch, just about to go inside, when the car had driven off the road, across the strip of lawn, and then had driven over the garden, mashing all the flowers. At first she had thought it was an accident, but the car had driven back and forth and back and forth, and she had heard them shouting and laughing to each other, enjoying their destruction with the kind of hysterical zeal of the very young or the very inebriated. The police said they weren't drunk — at least they hadn't been able to pin that on them. And they hadn't found any drugs. It was more frightening to think that there was nothing except pure malice, the kind of vindictiveness that comes from years of poverty and resentment.

The article in the newspaper the following afternoon had given the driver's name and address, and she had driven by his house. It was the sort of place she had expected: a neglected farm with a house half-covered with mustard-colored asbestos shingles, a tilting barn surrounded by pickup trucks in various stages of disrepair, a rueful dog chained to a tree that had been denuded by tent caterpillars. She had gone to have a look because she wanted an explanation. She thought if she saw the place where this person had come from she would pity him and perhaps understand. But pity is a fragile creature, easily contaminated by fear and then turned into anger. She had gone home and called the police officer back and said that, yes, she would press charges if they needed her to. They asked her to estimate the damage, and she'd said a hundred dollars. But how could she estimate the true losses: her labor, her time, her caring?

For a moment when she had watched them, she had wondered if they had been sent by Harold, but she had known, almost as soon as the thought had formed in her mind, that it could not be true. Harold had no reason to want to damage anything of hers, having already damaged everything that had

What We Save for Last

counted between them. She had not fought to save things, either because she did not have the proper fighting spirit, as her mother accused her, or because she did not really love Harold enough. Instead, she had fought to keep the house and had won. Harold said it was a mistake. He was certain she would not be able to keep it going. She had worked hard the past few months to prove him wrong. She still hadn't taken all the storm windows down, nor had she repaired the leaking gutters, but she had planted a flower garden in the front, a display of petunias, zinnias, marigolds, dahlias and snapdragons so profuse it was almost comic. If Harold ever drove out this way—she suspected he sometimes did—she was sure he'd see it. The garden proclaimed, "I've survived. I'm thriving. I'm happy." It was her brave, false front. When her mother saw the garden she said, "So you still want to get his attention, Jean. You still love him, don't you?"

But it wasn't love. It was a childish sort of vindication that had nothing to do with love. She had dug up a large area of lawn to plant the garden—a lawn that Harold had once maintained with the fervor of a first-time home owner. She had dug it up, bit by bit, taking each clump of grass and shaking loose the soil, like shaking someone by the hair. She had gone over every square inch with a hand cultivator, raking out all the roots and stones. She was too impatient to start plants by seed. She had gone to greenhouses and roadside nurseries and spent an exorbitant amount of money on flats of annuals, and she had set them in the ground. It was a cheater's garden, but it was so dazzling she didn't care. She had never given in to impatience, never indulged herself quite so thoroughly before. She had been raised to believe that such indulgence would be paid for by guilt. But so much for that careful upbringing, all those years of admonishments; she had felt only satisfaction looking at her garden, no guilt.

They have spotted her in the garden. The two young men who were in the front seat start down towards her, slamming the car doors behind them. The third guy stands by the car, leaning against his open door. She has never seen their faces before. She had been able to make out three heads in the car that evening, nothing more.

The driver of the car is fat, with no neck and a low forehead and the nearly-naked head of a marine recruit. His buddy is pale and thin, with shoulder-length blond hair. He is dressed all in black. The driver is clearly the leader of the group. "Hey," he calls out, "are you the lady who lives here?"

She thinks about saying "no." Just because she is here, working in the garden, doesn't mean she lives here. Does not mean she is the woman who had seen their car that evening, called the police, put the police on their tail. The police had arrived with surprising speed, had spotted them, chased them all over town until they had blown a tire, then hauled them down to the station where they were videotaped, fingerprinted, and charged with damaging personal property, resisting arrest, disturbing the peace, and assaulting a police officer. She doesn't say anything at all, but the driver comes closer to her and repeats his question, almost as if he was not aware he had already asked it.

"You the lady who lives here?"

The blond guy consults a slip of paper he produces from his pocket. "Make sure, first," he hisses at the driver. "Make sure we got the right one." He looked tough until he opened his mouth, but when he talks he reveals that he is missing a few teeth, and the remaining ones are tiny and pointy, as if he suffered malnutrition as a child. He hands the piece of paper over to the driver who squints at it, then looks up at her.

"You Mrs. Tobin?" he asks.

The police officer who had come to write up the report had called her "Mrs. Tobin," even though he had no reason to assume she was married—except that single women didn't usually own houses around here. Tobin was her maiden name, she'd never changed it, but she was too weary to correct him.

"Mrs. Tobin?"

"Yes," she says, softly.

"We got something for you, then," the driver says.

The blond guy looks back to the car. "Skeet should be with us on this," he says.

"Hey Skeet, get over here," calls the driver. "We're all in on this together."

Skeet is dark and scrawny, with ears that stick out like a coyote. They wait for him to join them. He skulks toward them, looking nervously at the road, then back at the house. He stops when he is a few paces behind the driver.

Jean holds her breath. It is unusually quiet outdoors. There is no sound of a car coming along the road, no sound of a chain saw in the distance. Jean knows that if she screams, there is no one around to hear her.

Harold had said this was no house for a woman alone. She had been too stubborn to agree with him. It had been an unlikely enough house for the two of them, academics living in a part of the countryside beyond the realm of the university. They had bought it soon after they moved to town, before they had any sense of its remoteness. Jean had taken a year to get used to living out in the country, and after Harold left she had to begin all over again. By day the little farmhouse has a pastoral sweetness to it, but at night it is creaky and vulnerable. There is a conspiracy of birds that keeps Jean awake—owls and nighthawks after sundown, songbirds at sunrise. But it is people Jean is most afraid of. She is uneasy when cars come along the road late at night, when they seem to be slowing down near her house. Now she strains for the sound of an approaching car.

"We got something for you," says the driver, stepping close enough to her so she can smell his body—an odor of cigarettes and gasoline. She looks past his shoulder at the third guy, who reluctantly makes eye contact with her, then turns away. An unwilling witness. She looks at the face in front of hers. It is a bloated face, with small, closely set eyes and eyebrows growing together over the bridge of the flat nose. The eyes do not blink. Jean feels dizzy and closes her eyes for a minute, but when she opens them again nothing has changed.

She thinks: if only I hadn't called the police, if only I had just let them drive away, if only I had just accepted what happened, if only I had been a passive receptacle for their meanness and spite and destructiveness. If only. If only she had known how it would turn out, she thinks, she would never have so much as protested. But before that thought is fully formed in her mind, it changes, she changes and feels a spark of protest rise up inside her. It is probably misplaced protest—protest against Harold, leaving her, allowing all this to happen—but it turns into something she has never felt before, a kind of separateness from her body, from her fate. Something like courage or defiance. It was right there, right beneath the surface, closer than she had ever imagined. And now it bathes over her. It astonishes her, this feeling of bravery. She had always thought it the property of other people, not of someone like herself. She had never known how accessible it was, how close a neighbor it was to fear.

"We got something for you," says the driver, once again, and he hitches up his shoulder and reaches down into his pocket. She stands right where she is, staring at him.

The driver is shoving something into her hands. She looks down slowly. She is holding a wad of money.

"Don't forget the receipt," says the blond guy. "We need to get a receipt."

The driver forages in his pocket and pulls out a folded piece of paper, which he smooths out and hands to her. She drops the trowel to the ground and takes the paper. She reads: "I have received $100 from Frank Judd in repayment for damages done to my property the evening of June 6th." The blond guy steps forward and offers her a pen and a cigarette box to lean on while she signs her name. The ink doesn't come out of the pen until the third letter.

Then they are off. She hears them slam the car doors, start up the engine, screech out of her driveway. In her hand are five twenty dollar bills. One of them is weatherbeaten and dirty, the other four are mint new and stick together.

She had not realized it, but she has been weeping. The tears surprise her when they fall on her arm, the back of her hand. She does not feel she is crying; they seem to be tears coming from someone else's face. She sits down on the ground, right where she is, in the garden. She feels as if she has been on her feet for a long, long time.

What We Save for Last

The Dream Broker

It had a hundred things wrong with it, but it was the right house. I knew it as certainly as I had known about Jules the first time I'd laid eyes on him, a decade before. There had been a few thousand students milling around in the half-light of the college fieldhouse, where registration tables were set up on the dirt floor. I had noticed Jules as I was making my way towards the table marked "Modern Languages." I watched him as he stood leafing through the course catalogue, instantly pictured our life together, and with uncharacteristic forwardness I approached him and said hello.

Jules was not indifferent to houses, but he was less passionate about them than I. His vision of an ideal house was unspecific. But I wanted a house set on a curve of hillside so it had two kinds of views, one close, one far. I wanted many-paned windows with old glass that would catch the light in different ways. I wanted a stairway with a bannister that was smooth under my hand, smoothed by generations of other hands. And I wanted a lilac bush by the front door, tall enough so that in the spring you could smell the lilacs from the bedroom window above.

If we were serious about finding a house, our friends informed us, we had better work with an agent. And if we wanted a house anywhere in the area, we'd better get in touch with Martin Shumetski. We were told he knew about properties for sale, even before the owners who planned to sell them. The Shumetskis had been farmers in the region for two hundred years, and still controlled much of the land, selling off their own acres slowly and cleverly. There was a raft of brothers and cousins, and among them they owned almost all the businesses in town. There was even a Shumetski Street, down by the railroad tracks, where a cousin had established a farmers' supply company. Now it was a flourishing, computer-run business, although it was still housed in the original nineteenth-century building with a sloping front porch and a woodstove in the front office.

I didn't trust Martin Shumetski from the moment I met him. He was a short, husky man with no waist and no neck. He wore short-sleeved shirts, even in cold weather, and his arms were surprisingly thin and hairless. He probably wasn't more than forty, but he was nearly bald, and he cleared his throat all the time when he spoke.

At our first interview I described my house to him—at least I tried to give him an idea of the sort of place I dreamed about—of course feeling foolish as I did so. Martin Shumetski sat there nodding non-committally, but when he heard our price range his head started moving side to side instead of up and down, without missing a beat.

"Well," he said at last, "I'll show you what we have. It's slow this time of year, but if you don't see what you want now, doesn't mean it won't turn up later. Though in your case . . ." He swiveled towards the file cabinets behind his desk, opened and closed a drawer without looking in it, and swiveled back to face us.

"What kind of hurry are you folks in?"

We were in no real hurry at all, except the hurry of desire. The apartment we rented was comfortable enough. Once we'd started thinking about owning a house, though, the apartment seemed plagued with defects, not the smallest being our neighbors' daughter, who had been practicing "Für Elise" on the piano for the past two months.

"No real hurry," said Jules, "but it would be nice to find a place before the spring."

"This spring?" asked Martin Shumetski. We nodded. "Well, in that case," he said, "we better get right to work."

When I say that I didn't trust Martin Shumetski, I don't mean to imply he didn't know the business. Perhaps the problem was that he knew it too well. He was familiar with every acre in the township. He knew who owned each house, how much they had bought it for, and how much money they had invested in it since. He knew which areas were going to be developed, which dirt roads were going to be paved, and where the power company was planning to string its new high-tension lines.

Once a week we'd meet Martin Shumetski in the parking lot behind the Shumetski Building, the two-story brick edifice that housed his brother's insurance agency, his in-laws' shoe store, and his own real estate office, its front window decorated with faded Polaroid pictures of various houses with SOLD written across them in magic marker. We'd get into his twelve-year-old Lincoln convertible and go house-hunting. When he drove, Martin Shumetski would look anywhere except ahead of him, as he filled us in with ceaseless anecdotes about the country folk. He always gestured around him with his cigar, an appendage which he sucked but rarely smoked.

The first weekend we saw a split-level in a development bordering a gravel pit. The next weekend we were shown a Victorian next door to the funeral parlor and a farm house next to the interstate.

"I'm just narrowing things down," Martin Shumetski assured us.

"We were hoping for something with a view," I said.

The next weekend we were taken to an owner-built house, which, from the distance, looked architecturally interesting. It did, in fact, have a beautiful view of rolling hills. But the owner-builder obviously hadn't known that untreated plywood has a tendency to warp, and the house looked as if it might not survive the winter. Martin Shumetski said nothing during the entire house tour beyond labeling the rooms as we walked through them, but he kept a close watch on our faces.

The next weekend he brought us to a sturdy white Cape. It was perfectly centered in its quarter-acre plot, and it had six evergreen shrubs symmetrically placed on the front lawn and trimmed within an inch of their lives. The rooms inside were tiny and excruciatingly clean. The owner, a little man in a meticulously ironed shirt, followed us around, proudly exposing the order in his narrow closets, and rubbing any remnants of our footsteps from the highly polished linoleum floors.

And so it went like that. Each week we saw more houses, and

each house was wrong in a new and unpredictable way. Occasionally Jules and I asked Martin Shumetski about some houses that weren't on his list, houses we had seen advertised in the paper, but he always assured us they were flawed in some vital way. One had septic system woes; another, termites; another, asbestos insulation. One that had no physical ills had a lien against the property that could never be resolved.

Jules and I got increasingly discouraged, but Martin Shumetski was perennially optimistic. He told us we were making real progress and acted as if things were moving along according to some invisible master plan. We were losing our faith in Martin Shumetski, but we didn't know where to turn. Our friends assured us that he controlled most of the good listings in the area, and if we temporarily defected to another agent, Martin Shumetski would never do business with us again. And Martin Shumetski had developed a formula that kept us in his power. At the end of each unsuccessful excursion, he would consult his notebook and murmur something about the property he hoped to be able to show us next time. And every Wednesday, when he called to set up our Saturday meeting time, he would mention some enticing aspect about the next place. The pattern kept us going week after week.

Between ourselves, we dealt with Martin Shumetski by reducing him to parody. We did Martin Shumetski imitations—hunching our shoulders, sticking our bellies out, clearing our throats—and made each other laugh. But the cycle of hope and disappointment was exhausting us. We thought about and talked about houses all the time. We lived in a state of excitement from Wednesday till Saturday, and then in a state of misery from Saturday till the Wednesday next.

In bed at night we found we had arrived at a kind of physical neutrality. The erotic desire that had sustained itself through our years of marriage had been supplanted by our desire for a house. I tried to think of Jules as I had once thought of him. I tried to recreate how I had felt when I first knew him, but the figure and the feeling had grown more and more remote.

One night, both of us lying awake, pretending we were asleep in case the other really was, Jules suddenly turned to me.

"I think we should give up on it," he said. "We've been looking for weeks and weeks and nothing's even come close."

"You mean we'll just stay here?"

"It's not so bad," said Jules.

"That's true," I said. I thought for a moment. "But who's going to call Martin Shumetski and tell him?"

"We won't call him," said Jules, his hand moving along my shoulder. "We'll wait till Wednesday when he calls us."

"But what if something wonderful turns up?"

"Wonderful it will be, except for the swamp in the basement or the kennel next door," said Jules, ending the conversation with his hands on my breasts.

But Martin Shumetski didn't call on Wednesday. We were home all evening and he didn't call. On Thursday he didn't call, either. He'd always been so regular; it was uncanny and unsettling that he shouldn't call this once.

On Friday evening, just as we were sitting down to dinner, Martin Shumetski was on the phone. He had the perfect property for us, he said. It probably wouldn't last on the market more than a day. If we met him in the parking lot at nine the next morning, he might be able to show it to us.

"All right," Jules whispered to me, while I covered the phone, "but this is the last time."

When we got to the meeting place the next morning, Martin Shumetski was standing by his Lincoln, shaking his head. He was terribly sorry, he told us, but there were last-minute problems with the seller, and we wouldn't be able to get in to see the place till the following day.

Jules would have started right back to our car, except Martin Shumetski touched his sleeve.

"I do have a picture of the place," he said. "It will give you an idea of what it's like. It's a converted mill."

We followed Martin Shumetski into his office, and he produced a black-and-white photograph. It showed a frame building with a massive stone foundation that was set on the edge of a small waterfall.

"It was renovated in the sixties," said Martin Shumetski. "Inside there's a two-story cathedral living room, a paneled study, a galley kitchen, a dining area with stone fireplace, two bedrooms upstairs, and two baths." His pinky darted about the photograph. He did not say charming or romantic or picturesque. I realized that Martin's great genius was his abstinence from adjectives. Every description was flat, seemingly objective, but he structured things so that you would supply the unspoken adjectives for yourself.

I gave Jules my all-purpose pleading look. "Well," he said, "it's not quite what we first had in mind, but I suppose it's worth a trip," and we set up a meeting time for the next day. All the way home Jules whistled tunes from *Die schöne Müllerin*, but that night he made me promise that this would be our last excursion with Martin Shumetski.

"I promise," I said, "if this house doesn't seem right — and in spite of its picture, I'm almost sure it won't — we'll tell him that we have decided to give up house hunting. I'll break the news to him as we're driving back."

The drive to the mill was through picturesque countryside, and Martin Shumetski seemed to have saved his best anecdotes for this trip. The mill turned out to be even more charming than its photograph. The view over the falls and the stream was spectacular, and the interior restorations had been carried out with care and taste. We could hardly blame Martin Shumetski for hoodwinking us into seeing this property, even though the mill was out of the question as a place for us to live. It had, I suppose, the sort of defects that are endemic to mills in general. For one thing, there was no place in the building where you could escape from the sound of the rushing water. All conversation had to be held at the level of a shout, and after we had toured the property for a while our heads ached. The other problem was moisture. The stream was set deep in a gorge where the sun was barely able to penetrate. Mildew had taken over the walls and floors and ceilings, and everything that wasn't stone or metal had begun to rot.

It took quite a while and a few hard glances from Jules for me to begin my speech to Martin Shumetski on the ride back. I told him that the mill was certainly an exciting property, but it wasn't really suited to our style of life. Then I began to explain that we had decided to curtail our house hunting for the present, but if we ever changed our mind and decided to consider purchasing a house again, we would be sure to let him know.

Martin Shumetski took the news with equanimity. He said he was sorry we were giving up just as we were so close, and then went on with an anecdote about a farmer he knew who had tried to use sleigh bells on the collars of his Nubian goats.

The trip back to the Shumetski building seemed longer than the trip out, and the landscape didn't look quite familiar. It occurred to me that Martin Shumetski was so busy talking he had inadvertently taken some circuitous route, but suddenly he pulled over to the side of the road and gestured out the window with his cigar.

"There it is," he said. "The largest maple in this area. I took you back this way because I wanted you to see it. Be sure you drive out this way and take another look at it in the fall."

I looked out the window where Martin Shumetski pointed, but as soon as I saw the tree, my eye was caught by the house beyond it.

It was a white farmhouse with faded green shutters and twelve-over-twelve glass-paned windows. It was set on the edge of the hillside with the sun in its face. I saw it and I loved it and wanted it with the same kind of certainty I had felt when I had seen Jules at registration those many years before.

"That house beyond the tree," I said to Martin Shumetski in a small voice, "you wouldn't happen to know if there's any possibility of it being for sale?"

As I look back on it, I see that Martin Shumetski had been manipulating us all along. He had not forgotten my first romantic description of the house of my dreams. He had stored it away and used it as the final stroke in his carefully laid plan. He knew about this house on the hill, knew that the old woman who lived there would soon be moved to a nursing home and the house would eventually come on the market. He knew, too, that it was more money than we were first prepared to spend, but that if we wanted it enough we would find a way.

He didn't pretend surprise at my question. He just cleared his throat and said, "When we get back to my office, I'll see what I can do."

It was almost spring when we first toured the grounds of the house. There was a brook and a duck pond. There was a pony-sized barn and a fenced field. There was a small orchard with apple, peach, cherry, quince, and pear trees in rows, five by five. There was a view of a flower border close to the house, and a distant view of the spires of the town poking out between the hills. There were no lilacs by the doorway, but there could be, I thought, some day.

Although the house was no longer occupied, we weren't able to get in to it for another week. Jules and I drove past a number of times and peered in the windows. The sun filled the rooms and the wide-board floors glowed like amber. When we finally got to tour the house I found it smelled as I had imagined — years of wood fires and apple pies baking. The bannister had a gentle curve and was smooth under my hand.

So we bought the house. We paid exactly what Martin Shumetski told us we would have to pay if we wanted to get it. We paid more for it than we had ever expected to pay for a house. We gave up all our vacations for the rest of our lives and took on a mortgage that would accompany us into our seventies. But the house, the house was ours.

I was right not to trust Martin Shumetski. He lied about all sorts of things. Rather, he didn't really lie, but he didn't tell us all he knew. He was, as we should have remembered, the master of omission. Once the closing papers had been signed and we took possession, we quickly discovered all the things he had neglected to inform us about. He hadn't told us, for instance, that the water from the well was thick with iron. He

What We Save for Last

hadn't told us that the upstairs had, for years, been infested with bats. He hadn't told us that the fireplace needed to be relined with firebrick, or that the patch job on the roof wouldn't last the season, or that carpenter ants were happily feasting on the barn.

If we had known about all these things we might never have bought the house. After all, there are limits to everything, even when you're in love. We were furious with Martin Shumetski and talked about hiring a lawyer, but by the time we had moved our things in and become acquainted with all of the house's recondite woes, it was already too late. The house had already begun to take possession of us, and we'd begun coping with the problems that had seemed so insupportable when we first moved in. We drank bottled water, paid an exterminator to deal with the barn, slept downstairs until we were able to persuade the bats to relocate, learned to shingle a roof. And so, without expecting to, we ended up feeling incurable gratitude to Martin Shumetski for his lies, his omissions. I am sure he kept the house's flaws from us because he knew they would frighten us away, and he knew that ultimately this was a house we would be happy owning. It wasn't that he took a personal interest in us and cared whether we were happy or not, it was that he was a professional who saw his job as matching up people and places, the way a marriage broker brings a couple together. He knew a perfect match when he saw one. If he knew there were things about the house that would cause us distress, he also knew there were pleasures that we still had waiting to be discovered: the breeze through the windows, sunsets and glimpses of the moon, the coolness of the basement, and the warmth of the hearth. And sometimes I think he even knew that right in the front row of the orchard, what the planter must have mistaken for a fruit tree sapling was in fact a large white lilac, full and fragrant as any I could have dreamed.

Corinne Demas Bliss grew up in New York City. She went to Tufts University and earned a Ph.D. from Columbia University. She is the author of a novel, *The Same River Twice* (Atheneum, 1982), and a collection of short stories, *Daffodils or the Death of Love* (University of Missouri Press, 1983). Her newest book, *Matthew's Meadow*, will be published by Harcourt, Brace, Jovanovich, Inc. in the spring of 1992. Bliss lives in the Pioneer Valley in Massachusetts and is an associate professor of English at Mount Holyoke College.

WHAT WE SAVE FOR LAST
was designed by R. W. Scholes,
typeset in Bem
by Stanton Publications,
and printed on acid-free Glatfelter
by Edwards Brothers.